AN INDEPENDENT MISS

"Do you view every man you meet as a challenge of some sort? As someone you must defeat, whether by outracing him astride a steed or outshooting him in an archery contest or in a battle pitting your knowledge against his?"

How outrageous he was. Stung by the injustice of his accusations, Justine said, "I happen to be quite satisfied with the way I am and so I have no intention of trying to change. Not for you or for anyone else."

When he stepped toward her, a looming dark silhouette, his expression hidden by the darkness, her breath caught and her pulse raced. "If you—" she began but had to stop in a vain attempt to compose herself enough to keep her voice level. "If you find me so lacking in feminine traits," she asked, "why do you even bother wasting your valuable time trying to improve me?"

Quentin sighed. "Because," he said, "for some reason I seem unable to help myself."

Reaching to her, he took her hand in his and started to raise her gloved palm to his lips. Justine snatched her hand away. She felt his hands close on her waist, his fingers almost circling her body. Even as she tugged at his wrists to push him away, he gathered her into his arms, his fingers sliding up her back to caress the nape of her neck. His lips brushed her cheek before closing over her mouth in a demanding kiss . . .

ELEGANT LOVE STILL FLOURISHES —
Wrap yourself in a Zebra Regency Romance.

A MATCHMAKER'S MATCH   (3783, $3.50/$4.50)
by Nina Porter

To save herself from a loveless marriage, Lady Psyche Veringham pretends to be a bluestocking. Resigned to spinsterhood at twenty-three, Psyche sets her keen mind to snaring a husband for her young charge, Amanda. She sets her cap for long-time bachelor, Justin St. James. This man of the world has had his fill of frothy-headed debutantes and turns the tables on Psyche. Can a bluestocking and a man about town find true love?

FIRES IN THE SNOW   (3809, $3.99/$4.99)
by Janis Laden

Because of an unhappy occurrence, Diana Ruskin knew that a secure marriage was not in her future. She was content to assist her physician father and follow in his footsteps . . . until now. After meeting Adam, Duke of Marchmaine, Diana's precise world is shattered. She would simply have to avoid the temptation of his gentle touch and stunning physique — and by doing so break her own heart!

FIRST SEASON   (3810, $3.50/$4.50)
by Anne Baldwin

When country heiress Laetitia Biddle arrives in London for the Season, she harbors dreams of triumph and applause. Instead, she becomes the laughingstock of drawing rooms and ballrooms, alike. This headstrong miss blames the rakish Lord Wakeford for her miserable debut, and she vows to rise above her many faux pas. Vowing to become an Original, Letty proves that she's more than a match for this eligible, seasoned Lord.

AN UNCOMMON INTRIGUE   (3701, $3.99/$4.99)
by Georgina Devon

Miss Mary Elizabeth Sinclair was rather startled when the British Home Office employed her as a spy. Posing as "Tasha," an exotic fortune-teller, she expected to encounter unforeseen dangers. However, nothing could have prepared her for Lord Eric Stewart, her dashing and infuriating partner. Giving her heart to this haughty rogue would be the most reckless hazard of all.

A MADDENING MINX   (3702, $3.50/$4.50)
by Mary Kingsley

After a curricle accident, Miss Sarah Chadwick is literally thrust into the arms of Philip Thornton. While other women shy away from Thornton's eyepatch and aloof exterior, Sarah finds herself drawn to discover why this man is physically and emotionally scarred.

Available wherever paperbacks are sold, or order direct from the Publisher. Send cover price plus 50¢ per copy for mailing and handling to Zebra Books, Dept. 4441, 475 Park Avenue South, New York, N.Y. 10016. Residents of New York and Tennessee must include sales tax. DO NOT SEND CASH. For a free Zebra/Pinnacle catalog please write to the above address.

A
Beguiling Intrigue

Olivia Sumner

ZEBRA BOOKS
KENSINGTON PUBLISHING CORP.

ZEBRA BOOKS are published by

Kensington Publishing Corp.
475 Park Avenue South
New York, NY 10016

Zebra and the Z logo Reg. U.S. Pat & TM Off.

First Printing: January, 1994

Printed in the United States of America

One

"First of all," Quentin Fletcher, Marquess of Devon, said, "I must get the kiddies off the street."

He proceeded to lead out his trumps with confidence, followed this with a daring finesse and then splayed the last of his cards face up on the table as he claimed the remainder of the tricks.

"Damnation!" Lord Alton threw his cards down on the green felt. "Never in my life have I witnessed such an astounding run of luck."

Quentin smiled, perhaps a trifle smugly, but made no reply as he collected his winnings from Mr. Ogden Stewart and Ogden's nephew, John Willoughby. When he turned to Lord Alton, the other man frowned. "I seem to have none of the ready at hand, Devon," he said. "If you would be so kind as to allow me to settle with you tomorrow evening at the Jockey Club . . . ?"

Quentin raised an eyebrow ever so slightly. "Of course," he agreed, though well aware of Alton's reputation for being a man with deep pockets but exceedingly short arms. Bidding his three companions good-night, Quentin threaded his way among the gaming tables to the door, nodding right and left when hailed by friends and acquaintances.

After he left, White's seemed strangely diminished.

Leaving the gaming tables, Ogden Stewart, Willoughby and Lord Alton repaired to the smoking room where they settled in armchairs for a bout of semiserious drinking. Alton, a fox-faced young gentleman dressed in the height of fashion, lit one of the Cuban cigars he favored, leaned his head back and blew smoke rings toward the high ceiling of the club. "That gentleman," he said, "is in dire need of a comedown."

Mr. Ogden Stewart, who was considerably older than his companions, blinked rheumy eyes. "Who?" he asked. Ogden, his thoughts, as usual, more on the rose-tinted past than the prosaic present, was renowned for his ability to misinterpret even the most obvious remark.

"Devon, of course. He considers himself to be much too much of a good thing."

"Because he happens to be devilishly good at cards?" Willoughby asked.

"Not only because of his luck at whist," Alton said. "A string of successes, however undeserved they may be, corrodes a man's character. He becomes toplofty."

"Quentin is more than merely lucky," Willoughby protested, "though I grant you he is that. He not only has a way with cards and dice but with horses as well. Not to mention women." Noticing the scowl that darkened Lord Alton's face, he added hastily, "Sorry." An amiable though careless young man, Willoughby spent much of his time smoothing unintentionally ruffled feathers.

Alton dismissed the apology with a wave of his hand.

"Sorry about what?" Ogden asked querulously. "Why must you young chaps constantly talk in riddles? How can you expect me to carry on an intelligent conversation with you if you refuse to speak plain and simple English?"

Willoughby frowned in a speaking way at his uncle, his look warning him not to pursue the matter. "I only meant to defend Quentin," Willoughby said, turning to Alton, "from the charge that his many successes are merely the result of the favor of the gods. After all, I consider him one of my best friends."

"A best friend!" Alton said scornfully. "And yet I know for a fact that you have no notion where he goes or what he does when he mysteriously disappears from town for weeks at a time. In my opinion, Devon has a choice bit of muslin hidden away in the country."

"I still fail to understand," Ogden persisted, "why you, Willoughby, felt called upon to apologize to Alton."

Willoughby shook his head, sighing in exasperation.

"He suspected he might have offended me," Alton said, "by claiming Devon has a way with women." When Ogden still looked puzzled, he added, "Because of that unfortunate Serpentine affair."

"Devon *is* a handsome devil," Ogden said. "And quite the charmer when he has a mind to be."

Alton sniffed. "I expect a woman might consider him handsome if she happened to have a taste for tall, fair men." Lord Alton ran his hand over his jet black hair. "But I fear his so-called charm completely escapes me. Unless his twenty thousand a year could be said to constitute charm."

"The Serpentine affair?" Ogden knitted his brow. Neither Alton nor Willoughby were surprised by the question since it was not uncommon for a considerable time to elapse before Ogden completely comprehended what was said to him and formulated an appropriate response. "Ah, yes, now I remember, that was the occasion when Lord Devon saved a Miss Georgiana Moore from drowning in the park." Ogden lowered his voice. "There were those who maintained that she threw herself into the water merely as a ploy to attract his attention."

"The whole affair was over and done with months ago," Lord Alton said. "Absolutely over and done with. It was no great thing so I no longer harbor hard feelings toward Devon, none at all."

Suddenly Ogden's eyes and mouth opened wide; he slapped his thigh. "By God, Alton, Georgiana was your *chère amie* at the time, and Devon not only plucked her from the water but snatched her right out from under your protection. Another example of the inconstancy of women." He glanced sternly at Willoughby. "That, nephew, was a most embarrassing subject to mention in Alton's presence. You young bucks should really be more tactful."

Again Willoughby sighed. "I intend to do my best," he promised.

"A capital resolve. Speaking of embarrassments, I recall the day Lord Kinsdale came to me—Lord Kinsdale? No, it must have been Prescott." Ogden ran his fingers through his thick white hair. "No, no, I had it right the first time, it was Kinsdale, without a doubt. At least I believe so."

"I was suggesting," Lord Alton put in hastily, "that our good friend Devon needs to be taken down a peg or two. He should be forced to eat a portion of humble pie for once in his charmed life."

"He *has* been acting rather high in the instep of late," Willoughby conceded.

"No, not Kinsdale," Ogden said more to himself than to the others. "Nor Prescott either, for that matter. It must have been old Riggs. Riggs happened to be a distant cousin of yours, Willoughby, if memory serves me aright. Passed on in the year nine, old Riggs did, at the age of three score and two. A fit of apoplexy carried him off."

"It would be for Devon's own good," Alton said, ignoring Ogden, "if we managed to hold the looking glass in front of him to show him he was a mere mortal like the rest of us. A good thrashing at the gaming tables might serve the purpose."

"We must do nothing malicious," Willoughby said. "I could abide a bit of sport at Devon's expense but naught that might do him harm."

"Certainly nothing malicious, upon my word," Alton said quickly. "You both know full well I bear Lord Devon no malice. A deucedly clever coil of some sort would suffice to put him in his place, a harmless prank and nothing more—something all four of us could sit here at White's afterwards and laugh about. As long as we three do more of the laughing than Devon."

"There were those," Ogden said, "who claimed old Riggs passed away after becoming overly riled by all the funning at his expense after his Indian Prince ran last in the Thousand Guineas' Stakes at Newmarket. He was odds-on, you know, and I myself lost a considerable sum when I—"

"That was many years before my time," Alton interrupted.

"Wait, my uncle may be on to something." Willoughby put down his glass of Madeira and leaned forward, lowering his voice. "We are all aware how inordinately proud Devon is of his Invincible. If we could challenge him to a match race with Devon riding Invincible and somehow manage to win . . ."

"Invincible almost lives up to his name," Alton said, "and I must admit Devon has always been a superb horseman. There might be four or five thoroughbreds in England who could defeat Invincible. But no more."

"Excalibur could best him. And I expect I might persuade Lord Clifford to let me run him against Invincible."

Alton shook his head. "To lose to a better steed would be no comedown for Devon. And he might very well confound us by winning. One way or another, most of Devon's ventures succeed in turning up trumps."

"Wait, hear me out. My notion is to disguise Excalibur by blackening the white blaze on his forehead—Clifford will fall in with the scheme, he enjoys a lark as much as the next one—so we could pass the horse off to Devon as an untried stallion fresh from the wilds of Scotland. Nothing would please him more than to best the Scots."

"Jolly good, Willoughby." Lord Alton rubbed his hands together in anticipation. "Now if only we could add a clever twist to the scheme, a topper of some sort."

Ogden cleared his throat. "Not so much because Riggs' horse lost, you know. Rather because the horse that outran him happened to be owned by a damned female." He put his hand to his chin. "Afraid I forget her name."

Willoughby nodded, started to speak and then stopped abruptly. He stared at his uncle. "Say that once more," he told him.

"Old Riggs never recovered from the disgrace of losing to a female. Nor would I in similar circumstances."

"Devon has a rather low opinion of the abilities of the female of the species." Willoughby steepled his fingers as he stared up at the haze of smoke hovering over their heads. "If he were not only to lose the race but lose to a woman, that would be a wicked comedown for him."

Lord Alton nodded. "We could always claim our horse was owned by a woman from Glasgow. Is that your meaning?"

"No, not precisely, I was thinking of our jockey. I propose our Scottish Excalibur be ridden by a woman."

Lord Alton considered that and then vehemently shook his head. "Devon would never consent to a match race against a horse with a female in the saddle even in the unlikely event we could find one to undertake the task. Never. The notion would be as beneath his dignity and as repugnant to him as it is to me."

"Agreed, he never would agree. But hear me out:

the jockey for our Scottish ringer would be a woman but a woman in the guise of a man. Think of it, Alton, picture the sensation when she whips her steed to victory, removes her cap with a flourish, allowing her hair to tumble down her back. I doubt if Devon would show his face in the *ton* for six months. Or longer."

"A capital notion with but a single flaw. Where on this earth would we ever find this paragon of a woman, one who could outride Lord Devon even if mounted on a faster horse? Answer me that, Willoughby, where is she?"

Willoughby slumped in his chair. "Sorry, I haven't the foggiest."

Willoughby and Alton sat in discouraged silence; Ogden, adrift in the past, stared beyond them. At last Ogden spoke. "He sired a daughter," the old man said. "Always wanted a son, Riggs did, but his only child, a child of his old age, turned out to be a female. A damn shame, if you ask me."

Lord Alton waved his hand. "If you please, Ogden, allow me to think."

"Never knew a man so desperate to sire a son," Ogden went blithely on. "Finally fathered a child at the age of fifty-three and what was it? A girl. He never accepted the fact that the baby had the misfortune to be female rather than male. Not her fault, after all. And so old Riggs managed to compound his wretched misfortune as the singleminded are wont to do."

"How was that?" Willoughby wanted to know.

"Old Riggs had decided to name his son Justin so he named the wee babe Justine, and after his wife died in childbirth he reared the young miss as though

12

she'd had the good fortune to be born a boy rather than a girl. None of your delicate needlework or daubing with water colors or fingering the scales on the pianoforte for her. No, by God, if she refused to be born a boy she could at least behave like one. So he raised her to hunt and shoot and do sums."

"I say!" Lord Alton was all attention now. "And this girl-boy, did he teach her to ride?"

"Damme, yes, he taught her to ride as good or better than any lad."

Willoughby nodded. "Justine, I recall her now, she must be a second or third cousin of mine on my father's side. I last saw her quite some years ago at a race meet, garbed like a young dandy." He frowned. "Surely she must be rather young."

"Never was much with sums, myself," Ogden said, "but old Riggs passed on eight years ago and so if I were to venture a guess as to her age I expect I might say seventeen or eighteen."

"She might be that by now," Willoughby said. "The last I heard of her she was in the care of an uncle of her mother's somewhere in the country. Near Gravesend? Yes, surely near Gravesend."

"Excellent," Lord Alton said, "she may well be the answer to our prayers. And since you, Willoughby, are a cousin of sorts, I suggest you be the one to proceed to the country in all haste to explore the possibilities." He gave a self-satisfied sigh. "If this scheme of mine succeeds, our good friend Quentin Fletcher, Marquess of Devon, will suffer a never-to-be-forgotten comedown."

* * *

On Friday of the following week, after receiving no reply to his letter to Mr. and Mrs. Henry Griffith of Gravesend, the couple he had learned were the guardians of Justine Riggs, John Willoughby boarded the afternoon mail coach and arrived in the port city shortly before five o'clock. A half-dozen sailing ships lay at anchor in the Thames waiting for the turn of the tide before sailing upriver to London.

After receiving several misdirections, one of which he suspected was quite intentional—as retribution for his showing no interest in a proposed visit to the burial place of the Indian princess Pocahontas, the supposed savior of John Rolfe, who had suffered the misfortune of dying in Gravesend while on the first leg of her return journey to America after a sojourn in England—he found himself, as darkness fell, walking along a lonely road on his way to the Griffith cottage.

Willoughby recognized the large oak described to him by a shopkeeper in the city—fortunately for him a full moon cast a bright, silvery glow over the surrounding countryside—and turned down a lane he had been assured would lead him to the Griffiths' and, more importantly, to their ward. Mr. Griffith, a cousin of Justine Riggs and not, as Ogden thought, a great-uncle, had been her guardian since the untimely death of her father.

As he hurried on, Willoughby, city born and bred, glanced uneasily at the shadows crouching on all sides of him. To raise his spirits, he began to sing softly, his voice rising plaintively as he came to the sad refrain: "But me and my true love will never meet again, by the bonny, bonny banks of Loch Lomond."

All at once he stopped, catching his breath as he

14

stood stock still to gaze in wary fascination at an apparition that seemed to hover above the field to his right. An apparition? What else could it possibly be? Willoughby asked himself, knowing that only a heaven-sent vision could be so lovely and yet so unearthly.

It was, he realized after a few minutes, a young woman gliding away from him as she climbed a low hill, a woman garbed entirely in white, her flowing gown silvered by the moonlight, her hair as black as the night itself. Though he was unable to see her face, Willoughby knew in his heart that she was indescribably lovely.

And he also realized to his dismay that in a very few moments she would disappear and he would never see her again. And he must see her again; fate, his romantic heart told him, had decreed that he follow her and discover who she was.

Without the slightest hesitation, he abandoned the lane and, after avoiding a fall into a ditch, strode into the field. For an instant he lost sight of her but, increasing his pace, he again glimpsed a shimmering wisp of white in the distance before his lady of the moonlight, as he thought of her, disappeared once more, hidden by the trees and shrubs on the hillside.

Willoughby hastened on, stumbling and almost falling before at last espying the dark ribbon of a path curling ahead of him up the hill. As he followed the path, he breathed in a faint, sweet scent. Wild roses? No, he told himself, nothing so prosaic, the scent was the perfume of the gods. When he reached the top of the hill, he slowed as he saw the dark outline of a structure some hundred feet ahead

The building, much too small to be a house, resembled a gazebo with a railed but unroofed porch going completely around, at least as far as he could determine, a one-story central section. There was no light in the building nor was there any evidence of the young woman he had followed.

What in the devil am I doing here? Willoughby asked himself as he stood staring at the building. He had no ready answer and yet he made no attempt to turn and retrace his steps. On the contrary, as though drawn by an unknown and incomprehensible force, he slowly approached the structure, peering ahead in a vain attempt to pierce the darkness.

Who was this young woman in her wraithlike garments? What had brought her to this lonely hilltop in the dark of the night? Perhaps, he thought with a twinge of jealousy mingled with a voyeur's guilt and anticipation, she had hastened to this secluded spot to rendezvous with a lover.

A twig snapped under his foot.

He heard footsteps from the direction of the building followed by the sound of a door closing. His heart in his throat, his pulses pounding, he held still, waiting.

"Who is it?"

The woman's voice was more self-assured, Willoughby told himself, than his would be if he were forced to speak at this moment. He stepped back, glancing around him for a refuge, a hiding place, finally sidling to his left as he sought to conceal himself in the shadow of a tree.

"Damn," he muttered as another twig snapped under his foot.

"Come forward and show yourself," the woman said, "or I shall shoot."

Willoughby drew in his breath in a sudden gasp. Shoot? This mysterious heaven-sent apparition was armed and prepared to fire on him? Impossible! He barely prevented a nervous laugh from escaping his lips.

A flash of light dazzled him. An explosion rang in his ears. A bullet whipped through the leaves over his head. Heaven-sent? She gave every evidence of being a demon from hell.

"Enough!" Willoughby cried, stepping forward into the revealing moonlight with his hands extended to his sides, his fingers spread wide. "I mean no harm," he said.

"Come closer," she commanded him.

After he had crossed half the distance separating them, she said, "Far enough. Stop."

He stopped at once and, in the ensuing silence, he sensed his unseen adversary appraising him. "Who are you?" she demanded.

"Mr. John Willoughby," he said, "of Woodstock Street, Mayfair."

"Willoughby?" Surprisingly, the tone of her voice made him suspect she recognized the name. "What are you doing here?"

"I was on my way to the Griffith cottage," he said as innocently as he could, "when I wandered from the lane and became lost."

"And what, pray, was your purpose in visiting the Griffiths?"

"Not so much visiting the Griffiths but rather to

meet my cousin, Miss Justine Riggs. I wrote to Mr. Griffith requesting an interview."

There was a long pause. Willoughby held his breath. "I happen to be Justine Riggs."

"Ah." For the last few minutes Willoughby had wondered if such might be the case. "May I speak to you here without fear for my life?" he asked. "Or, if you prefer, Miss Riggs, we might walk down the hill to your home."

"Since I rarely shoot kin, Cousin John, your life is safe," she said with amusement lightening her voice, "so let us talk here. The steps are to your right."

He made his way toward the sound of her voice, saw the outline of a railing and climbed the steps to the walkway. Justine stood facing him, one hand on the rail, her head uncovered, her oval face framed by curling midnight-hued tresses, her eyes seemingly as dark as her hair. She was even lovelier than Willoughby had imagined.

The sharp tang of gunpowder permeated the air but Willoughby saw no sign of the pistol, if a pistol had, in fact, been her weapon.

"Mr. Griffith is, to tell the truth, ill much of the time," she told him, "and tends to be less than hospitable to strangers, at least when feeling as poorly as he has these past few weeks. I expect he never replied to your letter."

"He did not."

"I offer my apologies for firing my pistol into the trees over your head," Justine said.

"And I regret having frightened you."

"You choose the wrong word, Cousin John. I may have been annoyed but certainly not frightened. Annoyed because you interrupted me before I had hardly begun." She turned from him to look up at the rising full moon. "Have you ever seen anything so beautiful?" she asked.

"No," he said softly and truthfully as his gaze encompassed both her and the moon.

"Let me show you a remarkable sight, Cousin John." Justine led him along the walkway to the far side of the small structure, stopping beside a mounted cylindrical object that tilted skyward. "Look through here," she told him.

Belatedly realizing that he stood in front of a telescope, he leaned down and peered into the eyepiece. A barren landscape in grey and black sprang into being before his eyes, a cratered sealike expanse surrounded by what appeared to be volcanic peaks.

"The mountains of the moon," she said, "and the great waterless seas."

He glanced at Justine and found her standing with both hands on the rail staring raptly up at the moon. Once more he became aware of the scent of roses. He made no reply; he wanted to remain here forever looking at her. After several minutes she frowned, perhaps becoming aware of his intent gaze, and turned to face him.

Caught off guard, he glanced away. "Your guardian built this, this celestial observatory, for you?" he asked to conceal his discomfiture.

"Oh, no. I did." He heard the pride in her voice. "At least for the most part. Old Mr. Jeffries from the village helped a bit with some of the heavier work."

Though he had been forewarned that her father had raised Justine Riggs as a boy, Willoughby was taken

19

aback to be actually confronted by a young lady who practiced carpentry and fired pistols at strangers! He most assuredly did not approve of such behavior and the fact that Justine was a bewitching lass made it, in his mind, infinitely worse. Her unnatural abilities made him feel uneasy, almost threatened.

"You came to Gravesend to speak to me?" Justine asked when Willoughby remained silent.

He quickly recovered from his bemusement. "I came hoping to renew our acquaintance after all these years. And to request a small favor."

"A favor, sir?"

Here was a young lady who would appreciate frankness, he decided. "This may appear to be a strange and presumptuous request, but I journeyed to Gravesend to ask you to ride in a race against a friend of mine. You do ride?"

She smiled. "I love to ride; my father put me on my first pony before I was two." Her smile faded. "You may be kin but I find your request somewhat startling. Do you actually expect me to ride a strange horse in a race?"

"Not only to ride but to ride dressed as a boy."

"How unusual."

Realizing how bizarre his request must sound, he went on to explain the circumstances as best he could. "Lord Devon deserves a putdown," he concluded.

"The notorious Lord Devon?" He thought he saw her grimace in distaste. "Even here in the country we hear tales of his escapades." She paused. "And where would this race be run?"

Willoughby had given no thought to that question nor, he was certain, had Alton. "In London? Certainly in London, perhaps in Hyde Park. Should you agree, my sister—your cousin Emeline Willoughby—has consented to be your chaperone."

He had expected to be compelled to convince the Griffiths to allow their young charge to accompany him to town, had even been prepared to offer them a modest monetary inducement to obtain their cooperation, but now, having met Miss Justine Riggs, he realized she would undoubtedly insist on making her own decision. Idly, he wondered if the courageous spirit of the princess Pocahontas had been reborn in this fetching though decidedly unconventional young cousin of his.

"London," she repeated. "When I was a girl, I lived in London with my father but since his death I have never even visited . . ." She let the sentence trail into a wistful silence.

"You would be afforded ample opportunity to view the sights." He had not the slightest notion what might appeal to this intriguing miss so he offered no specifics.

She turned away from him to again look up at the orb of the moon. Willoughby began to despair. "I assure you, Cousin," he said, "that your horse will outrun even Devon's Invincible."

Justine swung around to face him. "Then why do you insist on this masquerade? This wearing a boy's garb?"

"For a most important reason. You must dress as a boy because Lord Devon would never deign to race against a young lady. In fact, from what I have had occasion to observe of him, I suspect he secretly despises women despite the compliments he lavishes on them. I suspect he considers women to be mere baubles, ornaments, like pretty roses plucked and put on display for a brief time before being discarded and replaced with fresher flowers."

Since this characterization of his friend was somewhat exaggerated, Willoughby experienced an undercurrent of disquiet as he spoke, afraid he might be betraying Devon. But no, he decided, there was more than a grain of truth in what he had said. In fact, much more than a grain.

"Imagine Devon's consternation, if you will," he added, "imagine his chagrin when he not only loses the race but then discovers his vanquisher is a woman."

"I despise his sort," Justine said. "Nothing would give me greater pleasure than to journey to London to race against him. And, Cousin John, I fully expect to win."

Two

"What an ungodly hour!" John Willoughby said to his sister, Emeline, and Justine as he drove his landau into the park. Lords Alton and Devon had agreed to race at six in the morning when Hyde Park would be deserted. "I have never in all of my twenty-three years been abroad at this time of the morning before."

Justine watched Emeline pull her scarf tighter to ward off the damp chill. "All in all, John," Emeline said, "this is quite a preposterous scheme. I fail to understand how you inveigled Miss Riggs into being a party to it. Costumed as a young man, indeed!"

Justine said nothing since, truthfully, she was beginning to wonder what *had* led her to agree to ride in a race against Lord Devon. Granted, she relished the opportunity to visit London with its exciting hubbub and bustle and she quite liked her Cousin John although she had found herself wishing he would stand up to Lord Alton. Nor, since she had worn breeches many times before, did her riding costume discomfit her.

Even the thought of the race itself failed to daunt

her. In fact, now that it was only minutes away, Justine felt a pleasurable thrill of anticipation. She not only loved to ride, she had always enjoyed the challenge of competing with boys and she savored defeating them, which she often did. To outride the arrogant Lord Devon would give her more than a little satisfaction. She smiled at the prospect since, from what her cousin had told her, Devon had not merely crept into favor with himself over the years, he had run pell-mell into it.

Why then did she feel this sense of wrongness, of somehow being at sixes and sevens? Could it be because of her ominous dream, a dream that had haunted her for years, the most recent recurrence coming only the night before?

She had dreamed she was imprisoned in a cage like a beast in a menagerie. A throng of people stared between the bars at her, the men and women mocking her, the children hurling stones.

As she huddled in a corner of her cage, the crowd suddenly quieted, drawing back and then fleeing as a hooded figure brandishing a sword stalked toward them. Approaching the cage, the figure sheathed his sword. Taking a large silver key from his robe, he unlocked and opened the cage door. As she rose and reached out to him in gratitude he turned and relocked the door. Swinging around to face her, he slowly drew his sword. She shrank away. He strode toward her and she awoke with her own screams echoing in her ears.

Becoming aware that John Willoughby had spoken to her, Justine roused from her disturbing reverie with a start. Emeline still sat beside her but Cousin John stood on the ground beside the open door of the landau offering her his hand. Beyond him the grass glistened with dew while the trees in the distance were shrouded in the morning mist. News of the match race must have spread rapidly for, despite the early hour, spectators on horseback and in carriages waited nearby in expectant clusters, passing the time by making wagers on the outcome.

Justine focused her attention on John Willoughby, asking, "Would you offer to hand your jockey down if he were a young man?"

Willoughby stared, then smiled and shook his head ruefully as he stepped aside. As Justine was about to leave the carriage, Emeline leaned to her and whispered, "How I envy you your courage."

Too surprised to answer, Justine stepped to the ground and followed John Willoughby to a stableboy holding her mount beneath an oak. "Ah," Willoughby said, patting the horse's flank, "here we have Excali—that is, Bonny Prince Charlie."

Lord Alton hurried up to them, nodded perfunctorily to Justine, turned to Willoughby, looked back at Justine, staring for a moment and then shook his head as he again turned to Willoughby. "No one has seen Devon as yet," he told him. "Could he have gotten wind of my scheme?"

"Most unlikely," Willoughby assured him.

"Now then, Miss Riggs," Alton said to Justine, "let me explain the conditions of the race." He waved vaguely toward a large Scotch elm. "That tree marks the starting line; Willoughby here will begin the race by firing his pistol into the air. The course is a mile in length, more or less, well marked by red flags and with old Mr. Stewart posted at the finish marker. You had an opportunity to ride the Prince yesterday, I earnestly hope?"

Justine nodded curtly, barely able to conceal her annoyance at Lord Alton's peremptory manner. During her brief time astride Bonnie Prince Charlie she had felt a bond starting to form between the spirited horse and herself. She loved horses both for their own sakes and because riding always brought back fond memories of her father. What marvelous rides they had taken across the heath when she was a child! What good times they had shared!

"Ahh!" The sound, the simultaneous exhalation of many breaths, rose from the spectators gathered near them. Justine glanced over her shoulder.

At the entrance to the park, a lone horseman emerged from the rising mist. As the rider approached them, the rising sun broke through the haze to envelop him in its shimmering light so that, for a moment or two, Justine was almost convinced that he wore a silver coat of mail. As he drew closer, holding his black stallion to a walk, the glow—the strange aura—faded away to reveal a gentleman of the *beau monde* garbed in gray from his narrow-brimmed hat to his waistcoat and trousers. Though his face was in shadow, she had the impression of fair hair, high cheekbones and deepset eyes.

"Justine!" Willoughby hissed as he grasped her arm, turning her so her back was to the roadway.

Belatedly she remembered her cousin had warned her to avoid Lord Devon—surely this was Lord Devon riding toward them astride Invincible—prior to the race. "You must not under any circumstances," he had

26

warned her, "speak to him, or all of our efforts will have been in vain."

Resisting a strong impulse to glance behind her, she followed Willoughby to where Bonnie Prince Charlie now stood pawing the dirt of the roadway. With Willoughby standing by, Justine stroked the horse's neck, enjoying his answering nuzzle.

She ignored the murmur of men's voices behind her until one voice rose strong and clear above the others to say, "By God, Alton, do you mean to say you deny me the opportunity to greet my challenger?"

Justine tensed, waiting and listening, but Alton's response was too low for her to make out.

"Ha, now I understand your little ploy." There was the lilt of triumph in Lord Devon's deep voice. "You thought to catch me by surprise but, by God, you have failed. Failed utterly."

Justine heard Willoughby catch his breath and from the corner of her eye saw him stiffen with apprehension. "I warned Alton not to underrate Quentin," Willoughby muttered.

"You take great pains to hide the identity of your rider from me," Quentin said, "for the simple and obvious reason that he is, in fact, a jockey of some repute. You have brought a professional to race against myself, a mere amateur."

Willoughby sighed with relief.

"Who is your mysterious master of the turf?" Quentin asked. "Could he be none other than Mr. Tomas Rossini, the Tuscan magician of the whip? Or perhaps your jockey is Mr. Sam Chifney who intends to defeat me in the final few feet with his famous Chifney Rush? You need not answer, Alton, I have no hesitation in racing against your chosen jockey, whoever he might be."

"Whoever *she* might be," Willoughby corrected under his breath.

Lord Alton held both of his hands aloft. "Horses to the starting line, gentlemen," he called, "if you please."

Justine put her booted foot in Willoughby's cupped hands and swung herself into the saddle. When he offered her a whip, she shook her head. "I prefer to race without the whip," she told him.

He cocked an eye but made no attempt to dissuade her. "Remember," he said, "at the three-quarter mark the course veers sharply to the left before the straightaway two furlongs to the finish."

Nodding, she leaned forward to murmur words of encouragement in the Prince's ear as Willoughby took the ribbons to lead horse and rider to where the starting line had been drawn in the dirt of the road. The Prince seemed to understand what she was telling him for he raised his head and danced sideways before allowing Willoughby to lead him toward the line.

When Justine saw Lord Devon waiting for them at the start, she pulled the visor of her red cap down low on her forehead to shield her face while at the same time looking away. She heard Devon laugh.

"Do your damnedest to win, Chifney, or whoever you may be," he said in his low taunting voice. "The better the jockey I outrace, the more I shall savor my victory."

And if you happen to lose not to a jockey but to a mere female? Justine asked under her breath. What will you say then, my good Lord Devon? Even as she pictured his flush of humiliation, to her surprise a tremor of disquiet coursed through her. I should never have agreed to ride in this race, she rebuked herself as a long-held yet long-suppressed secret fear, a fear from long ago, struggled to surface. Drawing in a deep breath, she shook her head in an angry albeit unsuccessful attempt to banish her doubts.

"This is a girl?"

Even after all these years, Lady Golden's high-pitched cry of disbelief still echoed in her mind.

"Do you mean to tell me, Mr. Riggs," Lady Golden went on, "that this young dandy is your daughter and not your son?"

Her father had dismissed the incident with a shrug, but Justine had never forgotten her humiliation.

She had agreed to the match race against Lord Devon as a lark, as an escape from the dreary routine of her life at Gravesend with a cousin-by-marriage who resented her presence and her cousin whose "illness" left him, more often than not, besotted by drink. Now she regretted her foolish impulse to agree to masquerade as a boy. When young she had enjoyed the love and companionship of her father, believing she might lose that love unless she pleased him by behaving like a boy. But even then she yearned to be loved for what she was—a girl.

Very soon, whether she won or lost the race, she would be revealed as being female but remembered unfavorably by her cousins, John and Emeline, by Lord Alton and, yes, Lord Devon, as the girl who masqueraded as something she was not. Glancing surreptitiously from the corner of her eye, she saw Lord

Devon looking not at her but watching Willoughby as he loaded his starting pistol.

How handsome Devon was! She frowned, surprised at her sudden interest in this arrogant, blond-haired gentleman. She had never been partial to fair men, she much preferred to daydream about the dark brooding sort in the Gothic tales she read, and yet there was something about Devon that intrigued her in spite of herself. The fact that in a very few minutes he would see her revealed as an imposter and thereby, if he lost the race, adding insult to his injury, discomfited her more than she cared to admit.

"Are the riders ready?" Willoughby asked.

"Ready," Devon said.

At that moment Bonnie Prince Charlie, as though reacting to the excitement pulsing in the air, pranced a few feet across the line. Justine reined him around in a circle, being careful to ride away from Lord Devon and Invincible, until she returned to the starting line once more.

Willoughby raised his pistol and again asked if they were ready. Devon and Justine replied that they were. The gun barked and both riders urged their mounts forward at the same moment.

At first they raced side by side along the dirt roadway. Then, little by little, Devon guided Invincible into the lead but Justine made no effort to spur the Prince on, having been told by Willoughby that the Prince often lagged until the final furlongs.

By the time they thundered past the banner marking the quarter mile, Invincible's lead had increased to three lengths. Flying dirt stung Justine's face; still she held her horse in check. At the half-mile banner, Invincible still led but now by only the length of two horses. Slowly the gap narrowed to a single length, then to half a length.

Lord Devon raised his whip, striking Invincible's flank once, twice, three times, and the black horse responded, increasing his lead to slightly more than a full length only to hold there, neither gaining nor losing ground.

With the turn at the three-quarter banner just ahead, Justine swung the Prince wide to the right, away from Invincible, intending to urge her mount into his drive to the finish after they veered to the left and entered what she judged to be the final furlong.

Ahead of the racing horses she saw a barouche and pair driving toward them along an intersecting side road. She gasped in alarm. A man ran toward the barouche, frantically waving his arms, and the two carriage horses slowed. One reared, neighing in fright. Justine glimpsed an older woman huddled in fear on the carriage seat while the driver stood to draw back on the ribbons. To no avail—the panicked horses broke into a wild gallop along a path parallel to the improvised race course.

When she glanced at Devon she found him staring straight ahead, oblivious to the runaway carriage, as he again resorted to the whip. If the careening carriage was to be stopped, she must stop it. Without hesitation, she swung the Prince from the race course and urged him in pursuit of the runaway barouche, now some fifty feet ahead and swaying alarmingly from side to side.

Slapping the Prince's flank, she gradually gained, at last drew even with the carriage, saw the grey-haired coachman clinging to his perch, felt her cap fly from her head, the pins loosening, allowing her hair to fall down over her shoulders. She came alongside the galloping horses, leaned far to her right to grasp the reins, failed and almost fell beneath the pounding hooves, reached far to her right again, seized the reins this time, then gradually slowed the Prince as she held tight to the reins until the carriage horses came to a reluctant halt, puffing and blowing.

Waiting until the two horses quieted, she swung Prince around and rode to the side of the barouche. The coachman had left his perch and was sitting in the open carriage wafting a vinaigrette under the nose of a plump white-haired woman. A gold-headed cane leaned against the seat at the woman's side.

"Are you hurt, madam?" Justine asked.

The veiled woman, dressed in black as though in deep mourning, seemed not to hear. The coachman turned, stared at Justine, then said, "Pray excuse Mrs. Baldwin, she's been dreadfully discomfited."

"Is there anything I can do to help you, Mrs. Baldwin?" Justine asked.

The dumpling of a woman looked up and shook her head, her hat wobbling precariously. "Dr. Glaspell recommended drives in the park for the betterment of my precarious health," she said plaintively, "and you see what happened. Realizing how dreadfully crowded our London thoroughfares have become, I said to Rodgers, 'I shall drive only early in the morning when no one is about and thus avoid any possibility of an accident while at the same time escaping the strong and harmful rays of the sun. I hardly expected to encounter whatever it was you were about. Are you and your friends conducting a race meeting of some sort here in the park?"

"No, only one very foolish horse race. If I could be of assistance . . . ?"

"You, young lady, have done quite enough already. My nerves are frayed to the breaking point and so I expect I shall be confined to my bed for at least a fortnight. Dr. Glaspell, who is kindness and sympathy personified, has been treating my nerves with a variety of medications ever since dear Mr. Baldwin passed over, but even he has no conception how susceptible they are to the slightest upset."

Rodgers leaned toward his mistress and whispered a few words.

"A daring rescue, you say?" Mrs. Baldwin said. "An act of courage? That hardly signifies for she should have stopped the horses since she panicked them in the first place. Imagine, holding a race meeting in the park!"

Waving Rodgers back to his perch, Mrs. Baldwin straightened her hat, lifting her veil to reveal eyes of a startlingly bright blue set in a round, unwrinkled face. "Yet I suppose Rodgers is right," she admitted reluctantly to Justine, "when he says I should be grateful that you stopped the horses. I do thank you."

Justine reddened. Not from modesty but in anger. Her face glistened with perspiration, she was still breathing heavily, her shoulder ached from the wrench of grasping the reins of the carriage horses, and Mrs. Baldwin had to be persuaded to thank her, and doing it begrudgingly at that, for possibly saving her life.

"Why are you dressed as a boy?" Mrs. Baldwin demanded.

"Merely as a prank."

"A most unusual prank, I must say. And you should never ride astride, my dear, for the results are apt to be"—the older woman lowered her voice to a hushed whisper—"quite inimical to the physical well-being of a young lady such as yourself."

Justine felt her blush deepening to a vivid red.

"And what is your name?" Mrs. Baldwin asked.

"Miss Justine Riggs."

Mrs. Baldwin shook her head. "I am not acquainted with any family named Riggs," she said.

"Mr. John Willoughby of Woodstock Street is my cousin."

"Though I may have heard the name I have never met him, but if I ever do, I shall tell him exactly what I think of anyone who allows a girl to cavort about Hyde Park at this time of day masquerading as a boy. What folly!" She picked up her cane and tapped it impatiently on the carriage floor. "Home, Rodgers," she ordered.

The coachman nodded, raised his whip to the brim of his hat in a farewell salute to Justine, called to his horses and drove off. The last she saw of Mrs. Baldwin, the elderly woman was tilting her yellow parasol to ward off the rays of the sun.

Justine, both disheartened and exasperated, sighed. Swinging the Prince about, she came face-to-face with Lord Devon sitting astride a sweat-streaked Invincible. She was dimly aware of Willoughby and Lord Alton watching them from a distance but the two men made no move to approach.

Devon scowled at her. Despite being taken unawares, she met his gaze. Reaching to his waistcoat where normally he would have kept his quizzing glass, he shook his head when he realized it was not there. He dropped his hand to his side but continued to look down his nose at her as though, glass or no glass, he was quizzing an unwelcome and suspect intruder. After subjecting both her and her mount to a thorough and critical examination, he curled his mouth downward as though finding them wanting in every respect.

She started to rein the Prince past him but Devon swung his horse and blocked her way. "I observe that your friends were not content with a single deception," he said with scorn. "Your supposedly Scottish mount is obviously as false as you are."

At first she failed to understand his meaning but when she followed his gaze she was surprised to see dark rivulets wending their way along both sides of the Prince's head to reveal a white blaze. Was it possible that John Willoughby had misrepresented the horse as well as the jockey? Recalling his slip of the tongue, she realized there could be little doubt he had.

"And all to absolutely no avail," Devon went on. "You must realize, Invincible and I had victory well in hand."

"That is not true! You went to the whip much too soon. The Prince would have overtaken you at the finish."

Devon made a sound she could only interpret as "Humpff."

How angry he made her! "You may sniff and sneer as often as you wish, my lord, but you know I speak the truth."

"Not so. The truth of the matter is quite different.

When you realized you had lost the race, you immediately deserted the agreed-upon course to hare off in another direction. Ostensibly in pursuit of a runaway carriage but actually to avoid certain defeat."

So furious she could only shake her head, Justine felt the sting of gathering tears. No, she refused to cry. Lord Devon might infuriate her but, no matter how biting his words, she would never allow him the satisfaction of reducing her to tears.

"That is not so," she said between clenched teeth.

"Where, I wonder, did they find such a marvel as yourself?" he asked. "A young lady adept at playing the part of a young man." Devon leaned toward her. "Or does the deception run deeper than that?" he asked. "Are you actually a young man who is now playacting the role of a female?"

She gasped. *How hateful he is! If only I had accepted the whip from John Willoughby, how I would enjoy slashing it across Lord Devon's arrogant face.*

He raised an eyebrow and to her surprise held out his whip to her. "Is this what you want?" he asked. "Somehow I sense it is."

She grasped the lash end of his whip only to have him hold firmly to the stock and pull her toward him until they were face-to-face, mere inches apart. His eyes, she noticed, were green. He stared intently at her. Neither of them moved and, for a moment, beneath the anger written so clearly on his face, she detected another emotion altogether, something she had never seen before in all of her eighteen years, something that both stirred and puzzled her.

He released his hold on the whip. She looked down at it only to realize that, to her surprise, her sense of outrage had drained away. When he made no effort to take the whip, she let it fall to the ground, urging the Prince forward. This time Devon made no attempt to stop her. She started riding toward Willoughby only to veer away almost at once, knowing she needed to be alone.

Tears, so long held in check, streamed down her face, not so much of anger, as from a sense of emptiness, a desolation she failed to understand.

When Mrs. Prudence Baldwin arrived at her town house on Grosvenor Square, she retired at once to the room that had once been her husband's library. After his death five years before, Mrs. Baldwin had brought her favorite chaise longue into the room but otherwise left it unchanged. Not that she intended the library to serve as a shrine dedicated to her husband's memory, she told herself, but because she found the room restful. She could be at peace here, shielded from the outside world by the heavy velvet draperies and reassured by the familiar dark mahogany paneling, the deep armchairs, the leather-bound books and the lingering scent of her husband's tobacco.

She had no sooner finished a cup of chamomile tea and closed her eyes for a nap when there was a tapping at the door. How very unusual, she told herself. Sitting up, she said, "Yes?" and peered into the semidarkness as the door opened to reveal her coachman.

"What is it, Rodgers?" she asked.

"Beg pardon, madam, but may I have a word with you?"

"You may." How intriguing, she thought. Although

Rodgers had been with the Baldwins for many, many years, having been hired by Mr. Baldwin, she had never before known him to intrude on her privacy in any way.

Stepping just inside the room, he said stiffly, "I wish a word in reference to the young lady we encountered in the park earlier this morning."

"The young lady?" For an instant Mrs. Baldwin blinked in confusion. Her mind, occupied with worry over her various ailments and their possible cures, had little space left for anything else. "Yes, yes," she said, "of course, I recall the young lady."

"She prevented, I believe, a most lamentable calamity by the dashing way she stopped our horses."

"She *should* have stopped them since she caused them to bolt in the first place. As, I believe, I informed her."

"The fact is, however, madam," Rodgers went on doggedly, "she risked injury to herself to help you. And in return, I regret to say and I apologize for saying, you were most ungracious."

Mrs. Baldwin was too startled by this unexpected rebuke to reply.

"Besides being intrepid," Rodgers said, "the young lady appeared to me to be most amiable and attractive. Despite her rather bizarre costume."

"And what do you expect from me, Rodgers?"

"If I may take the liberty of offering a suggestion, madam, you should show your gratitude in some appropriate way. Not only do I believe so," he added with a significant glance at the portrait of the late Eustace Baldwin hanging above the mantel, "I'm certain if Mr. Baldwin were alive today he would whole-heartedly agree."

Mrs. Baldwin stared at her coachman, agape. "That will be all, Rodgers," she said, once she recovered from her shock at his outspokenness.

"Thank you, madam." Rodgers stepped back into the hall, quietly closing the door behind him.

How strange, Mrs. Baldwin said to herself, for Rodgers to take such an interest in that boyish young lady. She leaned forward, massaging her forehead with her fingers as she felt the first twinges of one of her dreaded megrims. She groaned, knowing that several days of the dismals were certain to follow the headache.

She shook her head. Life was entirely too complicated, what with one perplexity leading to another. For Rodgers was almost certainly right, Mrs. Baldwin thought as she looked up at the portrait of her husband. "Eustace," she said aloud, "you *would* want me to help that young lady, I know you would." She sighed. "And I shall."

When a man decides to assist a young lady, his first inclination is to give her money or else gifts purchased with money. Women, being more farsighted as well as more practical, focus their attention on much more important matters.

That young lady, Mrs. Baldwin told herself, should be properly married. Marriage will stop, once and for all, such hoydenish pranks as racing in the park; wild romps of that sort need to be curbed by a husband's firm rein.

Mrs. Baldwin frowned. Apparently Miss Riggs' family had failed in their most important duty. How regrettable. "Eustace," she promised, "I intend to come to her assistance as she came to mine. You shall see Miss Riggs wed before the year is out."

Three

"How can a man ever become sated with London when every turn in the street reveals a new and pleasant surprise?" Lord Devon asked as he and John Willoughby strolled along the Strand in the early afternoon. "Look, John, there we have an itinerant band; and here we have a barrel organ with its sportive, dancing monkey."

"The band happens to be loud and out of tune."

"True enough. But to me it sounds not merely loud but wondrously loud and not only out of tune but delightfully out of tune."

"Upon my honor, Devon, how uncommonly cheerful you are this afternoon. On any other day you would point out that the bands, the Punch and Judys and the white mice running in their twirling cages all serve to attract jostling throngs, and throngs are the perfect hunting grounds for pickpockets."

"Ah, but a pinch of danger adds spice to the feast that is our London."

"If you say so. What I say is that not only do Londoners risk having their pockets picked by roving thieves but, if they fail to exercise caution, they may well be fleeced by the mountebanks lurking on every other corner with their playing cards or some other game of chance—plausible charlatans ready to entrap the unsophisticated with their deceptions. Where does the pea lurk, Devon, beneath which of the three shells?"

Devon laughed. "At least I know the pea will never be discovered beneath the shell I select." He frowned and, when he went on in a softer tone, it was almost as though he spoke to himself. "Are we, though, any wiser than the most gullible lad from the country, we of the *ton* who lose thousands on the turn of a card at White's or on a wager made as the result of a whispered suggestion of a friend who claims to be an acquaintance of the uncle of the brother of a knowing trainer at Newmarket?"

"You exaggerate, my dear Devon."

"And how do you have the temerity, John, to denounce these petty deceptions after disguising that magnificent stallion Excalibur and renaming him Bonnie Prince Charlie?" Though Devon spoke in seeming jest, an undercurrent of vexation threaded through his voice.

"Not the same thing at all. The race in the Park was a prank, nothing more or less."

"And Alton's idea for the most part, I suspect. I can hear that nasal intonation of his now. 'Our good friend Devon needs taking down a peg, by God.' "

John reddened at the accuracy of his friend's thrust. "We intended no harm," he parried weakly.

"I must admit I found the girl disguised as a jockey to be a masterful touch." Devon paused to watch a wagon loaded with huge stones creak past on its way to the site of the new Waterloo Bridge. "How Alton would have snickered—you must admit he does tend to snicker when amused—to see me outraced by some mere chit of a girl. Not that I was in any danger of losing the race to your Miss—What was her name? Briggs? Griggs?"

"Miss Justine Riggs," John said.

"Just so. Riggs." As, Devon admitted to himself, he had been perfectly well aware. He pretended to examine the engraved silver head of his walking stick as he recalled, with bemused surprise, how often in the last few days his thoughts had turned, unbidden, to Justine Riggs. "A young lady from the country, I believe. And related to you in some obscure way."

"Miss Riggs is my cousin from Gravesend, an extremely distant cousin on my mother's side. It might interest you to know that only yesterday Mrs. Baldwin, the widow she rescued from the runaway carriage, offered to—But enough, Devon, I have no wish to bore you with trivialities."

Devon glanced from the corner of his eye at Willoughby, wondering how he could elicit the details of Mrs. Baldwin's offer without showing undue interest. "I detest mysteries," he said after a pause, "even trivial ones. What did the good Mrs. Baldwin offer Miss Riggs?"

"She most generously proposed that Justine come to live with her in town where she would sponsor my cousin in society—a most surprising offer from Mrs. Baldwin, since she has the reputation of being something of a recluse. I suspect her man Rodgers had a hand in it."

"Ah," Devon said, all the while wondering why he was so agreeably surprised to hear Willoughby's tattle? And why he was so eager to hear the answer to his next question. "And what, pray tell," he asked in his most offhand manner, "did Miss Riggs reply?"

"I fail to comprehend why you refused Mrs. Baldwin's kind offer," Emeline said as the two young women were being driven in an open carriage along Piccadilly on their way to view the nearly completed Waterloo Bridge.

Justine glanced at her cousin. "After meeting Mrs. Baldwin by chance a mere two days ago, her suggestion that I come to live with her in town quite surprised me. Though I found her most amiable and have heard nothing but good about her, she is still a stranger. I had no choice but to refuse." Even so, Justine acknowledged to herself, she had been sorely tempted by the widow's offer.

"I assure you, Justine, Mrs. B. is respectability itself despite her reputation for eccentricity."

"Eccentricity? In what way is she eccentric?"

"She acquires ailments as readily as you or I might acquire hats. Not just any ailments, mind you, she much prefers the most fashionable illnesses to the more ordinary varieties."

"Imaginary illnesses are certainly preferable to real ones."

"You should at least have given her offer serious consideration."

"Would you, Cousin Emeline, agree to live in

Brighton if a kindly matron you had met only two days ago offered you the opportunity?"

"Certainly not. But our circumstances are completely different since I care little for Brighton while you appear to be enamored of London."

Justine nodded in eager agreement. "In town everyone walks at least half a step faster than they do in Gravesend. And this morning I was wakened not by the monotonous barking of dogs but by delightful street cries of 'Peas green, Strawberries ripe, and Cherries red.' "

How tiresome, Emeline's glance seemed to say. "For myself," she said, "I would be absolutely lost without the London shops. I live for the latest fashions."

Justine sighed, wondering why she always seemed to say the wrong thing. After all, she did like clothes as much as the next one, as long as that next one was not Emeline. Obviously, Justine told herself, she thought more like a country girl than a sophisticated Londoner.

"How perfectly tedious the country must be if one is required to remain there all year round," Emeline said as their carriage swung into the crowded Strand. "Are you happy with your circumstances in Gravesend? I have the distinct impression such is not the case."

Justine bit her lip, not wanting to be evasive but unwilling to reveal the true extent of her misery. "I am not unhappy," she equivocated, lowering her parasol only to almost immediately raise it again. "Whether happy or unhappy," she said, "I will never accept charity."

She remembered her father telling her, after his fortunes began to ebb, "No Riggs has ever accepted charity and I refuse to be the first. I would rather die than be beholden to strangers; I would rather—" She realized his pause was to allow him time to find a phrase suggesting a fate even worse than death. "I would rather," he concluded triumphantly, "emigrate to the United States of America."

As she watched Emeline purse her lips in evident disagreement, the memory faded.

"Surely Mrs. Baldwin's offer would not be considered charity," Emeline said, "when in all probability you saved her life in a most heroic fashion."

The praise caused Justine to shift uncomfortably. "Anyone would have done the same."

"The fact remains that Mrs. Baldwin was saved not by just anyone but by you, Justine. Why, most young men, including my brother John—whom I love dearly—could never have stopped those rampaging horses."

Despite herself, Justine reddened at the suggestion that her cousin found her less than feminine. She glanced at Emeline to see if she had noticed her discomfiture only to find her companion looking elsewhere. When she followed Emeline's surreptitious glance, her heart leaped to see Lord Devon and John Willoughby strolling toward them along the walk on the other side of the Strand.

"I say, Devon, look there." John Willoughby nodded toward the bustling thoroughfare. "My sister did mention she and Miss Riggs intended to view the bridge."

"Miss Riggs? Where?"

Devon saw the Willoughby carriage, recognizing Emeline at once, but it was a moment before he realized that her companion, a young lady whose black ringlets framed an enchanting face, was none other than Justine Riggs. Though her high-crowned white bonnet appeared new, her white dress festooned with a bow of pale yellow at the throat had been out of fashion for at least two seasons.

"Absolutely stunning," John murmured as the two men raised their hats in salute. The carriage clattered past with both Emeline and Justine looking to their right, to their left, above and beyond them, but never at them.

"Damnation!" Devon slammed his hat back on his head and strode angrily on. "They refuse to recognize us. How tiresome."

"Never noticed us, I expect, in this crush," John said as he quickened his step to keep pace with his friend.

"Women see exactly what they choose to see, my friend, make no mistake about that."

"There are those who would say both my sister and Miss Riggs have good reasons not to acknowledge you."

"Nonsense. As for your sister, that unfortunate misunderstanding occurred more than a year ago. As for Miss Riggs, she has no reason at all to cut me." When John glanced at him in a speaking way, Devon said, "Unless she took umbrage at my fully justified remarks following our race in the park. Not that I was uncivil to her, mind you, I merely called attention to the fact that she had abandoned the contest to avoid

47

certain defeat. And I believe I made her aware of my knowledge of her double deceit in disguising not only herself but her horse."

"As a matter of fact," Willoughby began, intending to inform Devon that Justine had not been aware her horse had been disguised. But his voice trailed off and he scowled. What was the reason for Devon's sudden interest in Justine? he wondered. She was, after all, *his* cousin, not Devon's, and, in a manner of speaking, *his* protégée. His quite fetching protégée.

"You were about to say?" Devon prodded.

"I was about to remark that at times both your words and your manner are more intimidating than you may realize."

. "Indeed? What could possibly give you that impression? I always speak my mind, nothing more and nothing less. This world would be a better place if only more men would do the same. I detest deceit of all sorts, I abhor circumlocution, I refuse to waste my time mouthing frivolous and unwarranted compliments."

"Oh! An admirable philosophy, Devon! Yet when actually put into practice, this credo of yours might well be the very reason those two young ladies refuse to acknowledge you when driving by on the Strand."

"If they prefer the smiling insincerities of society, so be it. No matter, in a few days Miss Riggs will return to her simple country pleasures."

"And to her stargazing."

"Her stargazing? Whatever do you mean, John?"

"When I met her I discovered, much to my surprise, that she possesses a telescope mounted in a gazebo of sorts situated on a hilltop near her home."

Devon raised his eyebrows. "Mankind's past is buried beneath the earth in graves and ruins, beneath the sea in wrecks and lost cities such as Atlantis; our present is here on the surface of our planet like a blight for all to behold; therefore many leap to the conclusion that we must gaze overhead at the stars and the planets to find hints of our future." He waved his hand as though to dismiss the idea as misguided. "So Miss Justine Riggs purports to be an astrologer."

"I believe she would prefer to have herself referred to as an amateur astronomer."

"An astronomer? You must be mistaken, John. Surely you learned at Oxford that astronomy is the serious study of heavenly bodies while astrology is a mere frivolous speculation. It follows as night follows day that men must be astronomers while women interested in the heavens become astrologers."

"Devon, I wholeheartedly agree with you. What you say is certainly true as a generality but in this particular case you happen to be in error. You forget that Miss Riggs is no ordinary female."

"I must admit I took her for a young man when I saw her in her jockey garb."

"On the other hand, if only you had seen Justine as I first saw her last week when she glided phantom-like across the meadows. She was entirely captivating, a vision of feminine delight."

Devon gave John a sharp glance. Was it possible John was enamored with his country cousin? Normally, Devon would have been amused at the notion but for some unknown reason he found the thought strangely disturbing.

"This must have been on your journey to Gravesend," Devon said, "when you enlisted her as an accomplice in your deception."

"How truly sorry I am about that, Devon. You must believe me when I say I should never have agreed to help Alton with his scheme. My only excuse is my desire to be agreeable."

Devon put his arm around his companion's shoulders. "I forgive you, not once but three times over. You and I, John, have been true friends for more years than I can possibly count. You never fail to encourage my better instincts while forgiving my baser ones—and I surely must possess a few baser instincts, they claim everyone does. What could be a better definition of a friend? What more could I ask of you? If need be I would trust you with my life."

John shifted uncomfortably, first glancing at Devon and then looking quickly away. Almost, Devon thought, as if he considered himself guilty of some offense, some further deception.

"She had no knowledge of the horse," John admitted with a rush. "None at all."

"She? Knowledge of the horse? You speak in riddles."

"By she I mean Justine. By the horse I mean Excalibur. Alton—no, Alton and myself, I accept my share of the responsibility—never informed her that the horse was other than some ill-bred Scottish steed."

"So I *was* unfair in my remarks to her, she stands falsely accused." Devon, espying his opportunity, felt an unexpected frisson of anticipation. "Tomorrow I shall call upon Miss Riggs to plead her forgiveness for my false accusation." He smiled to himself as he pictured himself confronting Justine, imagining her unease as she awaited still another rebuke from him and then her surprise and delight when she realized he had come not to chastise her but to extend the most magnanimous of apologies.

True to his word, Lord Devon arrived at the Willoughby town house on Woodstock Street early the next afternoon. After sending his card up to Miss Justine Riggs, he examined his reflection in the drawing-room looking glass, nodding with satisfaction at what he saw there. Blue *was* his best color, he decided.

When John Willoughby's image appeared in the glass, Devon turned to greet his friend.

"Miss Riggs is not at home," John said.

Devon nodded. Something in John's tone of voice made him ask, "Truly not at home?"

"Not at home to you, my dear Devon."

Lord Devon stared. In high dudgeon, he flushed. "Be so kind," he said stiffly, "as to inform Miss Riggs that I have come to tender my apologies for certain inaccurate remarks I made the other day in the park."

"As you wish." John bowed and departed only to return in a matter of a few minutes. "Miss Riggs is not at home," he announced, suppressing a smile at his friend's startled discomfort.

Devon struck his open palm with his fist; he shook his head; clasping his hands behind his back, he paced back and forth in front of the fireplace. Slowly his anger at the unexpected rebuff cooled, giving way to annoyance. "The loss," he muttered, "is hers, not mine."

"Whether hers or yours," John told him, "I fear the

loss is permanent since my cousin Justine departs for Gravesend early tomorrow morning."

Devon smiled thinly. "Give her my best wishes for a safe and pleasant journey," he said. Clapping his friend on the shoulder, he strode from the house to his waiting curricle.

As he drove home, he considered taking a temporary leave from society to enter the secret and revivifying world of his retreat on Whitechapel Road. No, that would not do, he would not allow himself to be thwarted by a young miss, particularly by one from the country. Refuse to see him, indeed!

Yet she would leave town on the morrow and he certainly had no intention of pursuing Miss Riggs to Gravesend to offer his apologies. How it would turn her head if he did! There must, he told himself, be a better way. If anyone could concoct a scheme to accomplish his purpose, he, Lord Devon, could.

He began turning the problem over in his mind, examining and discarding one idea after another. And then, as he had been confident it would, a plan began to take shape . . .

As Justine busied herself with packing her portmanteau—no longer accustomed to having servants, she had insisted on making her own preparations for departure—she wondered if she had done the right thing in refusing to see Lord Devon. How she would have enjoyed hearing him admit his error! How she would have savored hearing him plead for her forgiveness! She had never met anyone who found so much in favor with himself.

Picturing their meeting, a confrontation that was, she imagined, destined never to take place, she smiled at thought of his feigned abjectness. If only—Her smile slowly faded and she sighed for all the "if onlys" of life. If only their stations were less disparate; if only she could be all he wanted in a woman—utterly feminine, garbed in the height of fashion, an aloof beauty worshipped from afar by all the gentlemen of the *ton*. Smitten despite himself, Lord Devon would court her, reluctantly at first but then, incited by her rebuffs, with growing ardor until he would at last propose marriage. And—how delicious the scene—she would reject him. Could her revenge be any sweeter than that?

How foolish she was even to imagine behaving in such a deceitful way, so contrary to her nature. She could be no one but herself, just as, unfortunately, Lord Devon could be Lord Devon and no other.

She thought of Lord Devon as a comet, a being who had hurtled into her life from the unknown, a brilliancy appearing without warning from nowhere to light the night sky as it hastened on its journey around the sun, a streak of light to be admired—or, perhaps, feared—from afar for a few days or a few weeks until it disappeared back into the unfathomable darkness of the great void of space, never to be seen again.

Except in her memory, where it would flame forever.

What romantic, sentimental rubbish, Justine chided herself. Lord Devon a comet, indeed! He had succeeded, however, in throwing her thoughts into a confused jumble. He was but a man, she reminded herself, and, if Emeline was to be believed, a less than admirable one at that. Even John Willoughby, his best friend, had hinted at grievous flaws in his character.

"After first being tricked by Alton and now scorned by you, Justine," John had said that very afternoon, "I expect Devon will disappear for a fortnight or more."

"To spend his days and nights with his bit of muslin," Emeline added with surprisingly bitter candor.

So Devon was wont to retreat in the face of adversity, Justine told herself with satisfaction. Hardly a heroic trait; in fact quite the opposite. Why, then, did he so occupy her thoughts during the day and, if the truth be told, her dreams at night? If his station in society was so impossibly high, which it was, and his character so woefully low, which it appeared to be, she should have received him when he called, accepted his apology, and dismissed him from her presence and her life with an indifferent wave of her hand.

Ah, but to have seen him again would have been impossible for her. No, not impossible, it would merely have been unwise. A comet is intensely hot, perhaps as devastatingly hot as the sun itself, and those who venture too close do so at the peril of having their wings charred, causing them to plummet back to earth. Shaking her head in exasperation at her tangled, perfervid imaginings, Justine stood and closed her portmanteau with unnecessary vigor.

At that moment there came a tapping at her open door. When Justine looked up she saw Alice, one of the Willoughby maids.

"There's a man asking for you, miss," Alice told her.

Her heart leapt. How persistent Devon was. "I am not at home to Lord Devon."

"Oh! Not a gentleman, miss, I didn't mean it was a gentleman. 'Tis only Rodgers, Mrs. Baldwin's man."

Puzzled, Justine descended the stairs to the drawing room where she found Rodgers, grey of hair yet trim of build, standing with hat in hand. His show of deference, however, was belied by the glint of shrewdness in his hazel eyes.

"Mrs. Baldwin sent you?" Justine asked.

Rodgers shook his head. "She has no inkling I am here nor, I trust, will she ever learn of my visit." His speech, she noted, was as refined as that of the quality he had served all of his life.

When Justine made no reply, he went on. "Mrs. Baldwin, I believe, offered to take you into her house and introduce you to society."

"She did indeed, a most gracious offer."

"And yet you refused to come to her."

Justine nodded, surprised by Rodgers's interest in affairs that appeared to be no concern of his.

"You were unwilling to accept charity, I warrant." Hurrying on before she had a chance to answer, Rodgers changed course. "I have come to add my thanks to those of Mrs. Baldwin," he said. "If harm had befallen her in the park, I could never have forgiven myself."

"You did all you could."

"I should never have agreed to drive the carriage that morning." Rodgers held out his hands; Justine murmured sympathetically when she saw how gnarled and twisted they were. "Mrs. Baldwin will tolerate

55

no other coachman than myself," he added, "despite these sorry hands of mine. And so I thank you."

"Anyone would have done the same," she said.

"That may or may not be." He bowed and walked to the door as though to leave, only to turn to face her once more. "When Mr. Eustace Baldwin, God rest his soul, lay on his deathbed," he said, "he beseeched me to look after his widow. Despite my best efforts, Mrs. Baldwin, soon after his death, went into a decline that has worsened with every passing year, until now I fear she will never escape her melancholia."

Rodgers drew a deep breath; Justine saw a tear glisten on his cheek. "I most humbly beg your pardon," he said in a choked voice, "but I possess a great affection for Mrs. Baldwin."

"If there was anything I could do to help her," Justine said, "I would."

Rodgers nodded. "Not for years have I seen her as animated as she was with the notion of helping you, Miss Riggs. Nor have I ever seen her so in the doldrums as she became after you refused her help." When Justine started to speak, Rodgers held up his hand. "Allow me to say that I understand your feelings perfectly," he said. "However, if you accepted her offer, you would not be receiving charity, you would be dispensing it—to an old, distraught woman who in all probability has very few years remaining on this earth. Pray reconsider your decision, Miss Riggs, I most humbly beseech you."

Four

Justine held her breath as M. Lambert, the French emigré employed as a tutor by Mrs. Baldwin to improve Justine's skills in art and music, peered through his quizzing glass at her latest attempt to create an acceptable watercolor. He placed the painting on an easel, stepped back several paces and, all the while frowning, tilted his head first to the right and then to the left.

"And what exactly does your painting represent, Mlle. Riggs?" he wanted to know.

Justine let out her breath with a sigh of defeat. "Ships anchored in the harbor at Gravesend," she told him.

"Ah, yes, now I begin to comprehend. Those undulations are meant to portray the waves. Is that not so, *mademoiselle?*"

Justine nodded. "Do you see any hope for me at all?" she asked.

"M. Lambert is always the optimist," he said. "With much serious study of technique and after much attempt and mistake, *mademoiselle,* you might, after the passage of several years, attain a certain competence."

Mrs. Baldwin bustled into the library. "Mercy, such a dreadful, dreadful summer," she said as she used a lace-edged handkerchief to dab at the perspiration on her forehead. "This sultry weather is much worse than any disease-bearing miasma. If only the rain would commence." Seeing the painting, she went to the easel, squinting as she leaned forward. "What a lovely scene," she said to Justine. "One must see many such meadows with their grazing cows in the country near Gravesend."

Should she laugh or should she cry? Justine wondered. Her innate good humor triumphed and she laughed. Mrs. Baldwin, smiling tentatively, looked puzzled.

"I intended my painting to be a harbor scene," Justine told her.

"I do suffer from rather poor eyesight."

"And I," Justine admitted ruefully, "suffer from a lack of artistic talent, as M. Lambert will be the first to testify."

"Your charming ward, however," he told Mrs. Baldwin, "does possess a most pleasant singing voice." Hearing the long clock in the hall chime four times, he said, "The time has arrived for M. Lambert to depart. Until tomorrow." Bowing right and bowing left, he backed from the room and was gone.

Justine walked to the window where she stood looking out at the gazebo in the rose garden at the rear of the house. The summer afternoon was hot and the air moist but, although clouds had cast a grey shroud over the city for the last several days, the long-threatened rain stubbornly refused to fall.

"My dear," Mrs. Baldwin said, coming to stand behind her, "you have no reason to despair. The ability to sketch or do watercolors is of little importance."

Justine shook her head. "If only those were the least of my failings. Not only is my artistic ability less than accomplished, M. Lambert must exert all of his tact and power of will not to cover his ears when I sit down at the pianoforte. As for my needlework, the less said the better."

"How unfair to yourself you are! You dance divinely, Justine, you speak French and Italian fluently, and I find you more than amiable. Your presence here has truly been a godsend."

Justine turned and, when she impulsively hugged the older woman, she felt a rush of affection when she saw tears glistening in Mrs. Baldwin's eyes.

"I fear that some gentlemen," Justine said after a moment, thinking of Lord Devon, "would be more inclined to label me waspish rather than amiable. Perhaps what I require is not so much the long-suffering M. Lambert but an alchemist of the social graces to somehow turn my baser qualities into golden ones."

"An alchemist?" After a moment, Mrs. Baldwin's thoughtful frown changed to a smile. "The very thing!" she cried. Seeing Justine raise her eyebrows, she hastened to add, "Not an alchemist—I have no knowledge of any alchemists practicing their art in London in this modern day and age—what we must do is consult an astrologer. And none is more gifted in interpreting the influences of the heavens than Mlle. Daphne Gauthier."

Now it was Justine's turn to find herself all at sea. "Whyever an astrologer?"

"After my dear Eustace passed over, I had the good fortune to be referred to Mlle. Gauthier who was able to reassure me that one day Eustace and I would be together again." She sighed. "That day, I expect, will arrive sooner rather than later since I was born on the thirtieth of June."

"An unfavorable date?"

"I had the misfortune to be born under the sign of Cancer. As you are undoubtedly aware, we Cancerians are prey to a astonishing variety of ailments." As she spoke, Mrs. Baldwin unconsciously placed her hand over her heart.

Justine, desiring to turn their conversation to a less distressing subject, said, "Though I happen to be a skeptic, I have no objection to visiting an astrologer."

"As I was myself before meeting Mlle. Gauthier." Mrs. Baldwin sat at the *escritoire*. "Please ring for Rodgers," she told Justine, "while I pen an urgent appeal to Mlle. Gauthier." After writing for a few minutes, she looked up. "I really should include the date of your birth."

"March twenty-ninth." Justine told her.

"And the hour? Do you happen to know the hour?"

"My father told me I was born a few minutes before ten on a Sunday morning. He always said the tolling of church bells announced my arrival into the world."

"Mlle. Gauthier will be most pleased with such precise information." Mrs. Baldwin was sealing the letter when Rodgers entered the library. "Will you deliver this to Mlle. Gauthier personally?" she asked him. "We intend to have a consultation with her as soon as possible." Looking up at Justine, she added, "I always worry so that my letters will go astray."

As soon as Rodgers left with a promise to personally place the letter in Mlle. Gauthier's hands within the hour, Mrs. Baldwin said, "Undoubtedly that explains it."

"I fail to understand."

"Being an Aries explains your unexpected refusal to see Lord Devon since an Aries is inclined to be stubborn. Some would even call them willful."

Had she been willful? Justine wondered. Perhaps she had been unwise as well. John Willoughby had predicted that Devon would drop from sight following her rebuff; he had not. Justine had expected him to return and again offer his apologies; he had not. Instead, Emeline had informed her, Lord Devon had gone about town as though absolutely nothing untoward had occurred, evidently having banished Miss Justine Riggs from his thoughts for good and all.

If only she, in turn, could banish him from hers! Even now she found herself wondering where he was, what he was doing and, she blushed to admit, whether his thoughts ever turned to her.

"A Mr. Rodgers is asking for you, milord."

"Ah, good," Lord Devon said. "Show him in, Allison."

When Rodgers entered the drawing room, Devon, who was standing behind a drum table, gestured toward a decanter of brandy. "Will you join me?" he asked.

Rodgers looked startled but managed to mumble his thanks.

As Devon poured the liquor into two large snifters, he said, "Damnable weather, this, the sort of dead calm you might expect before a natural catastrophe, a hurricane, an earthquake or the like." After handing one of the glasses to Rodgers, he raised his own in a salute to his guest and Rodgers bowed his head in acknowledgement. Both men paused to inhale the aroma of the brandy, both nodded with satisfaction and then sipped in silence.

"I understand," Lord Devon said, once they were seated at the hearth, "that you followed my suggestion concerning Miss Riggs."

"I did indeed, milord."

"And as a result she agreed to accept Mrs. Baldwin's more than gracious offer."

"She did. And now she is being instructed in all of the obligatory feminine graces." Rodgers swirled the brandy in his glass. "With results I can only describe as mixed."

"And Mrs. Baldwin?"

"Her health, recently so wretched, appears much improved."

"Capital. As I suspected would be the case, our joining forces has resulted in benefits to both of us. Not to mention Mrs. Baldwin and Miss Riggs." Devon placed his empty glass to one side. "You bring news, I assume."

Rodgers hesitated. "I wish to say, milord, that Mrs. Baldwin and myself find Miss Riggs to be a most warmhearted young lady, amiable and engaging. Mrs. Baldwin, in fact, has referred to her several times as a treasure. In the space of less than a month we have, in short, grown quite fond of the young lady."

"An admirable sentiment that does credit to you both, yet is hardly an explanation for your presence here today."

"I would not want harm to come to her, milord, as the result of any action of mine."

Devon's face clouded. "You forget yourself, Rodgers," he said angrily. "Are you suggesting by any chance that I might—?"

Rodgers drank the last of his brandy, placed the glass on the table beside his chair and rose. "I was simply stating facts while suggesting nothing. I wish you good day, Lord Devon."

"Wait." Devon also rose. "The fault is partly mine," he admitted, "for seeking your help while supplying no hint of my motives. No harm will befall Miss Riggs, I assure you. I give you my word on that. I merely wish to set matters right between the young lady and myself." Is that really all you have in mind, Devon? he asked himself. Are your motives of such a high order, are they so completely honorable?

Rodgers hesitated and then gave a nod of satisfaction. "Mrs. Baldwin," he said, "intends to accompany Miss Riggs to an astrologer for a consultation. Not only an astrologer, the lady in question reads palms as well." He touched the pocket of his coat. "I have with me a letter to deliver to a Mlle. Daphne Gauthier."

"Damme. So Daphne styles herself an astrologer now. If my father's tales about her contained even a scintilla of truth, she has a rather checkered past." Devon smiled. "At least time has broadened her celestial horizons. When she was young, she seemed to be under the influence of Venus alone, while now I suppose she must concern herself with the other planets as well. I wonder what your employer expects to accomplish by such a visit."

"I believe, milord, that madam hopes that Mlle. Gauthier's knowledge of planetary influences will reveal a suitable attachment for Miss Riggs."

Devon felt a painful stab in the vicinity of his heart. "Balderdash!" he cried. "How absurd. An amateur astronomer placing herself in the hands of an astrologer to provide herself with a suitable mate?" He must, Devon told himself, protect this country miss from the well-meaning yet dangerous plans of a benefactor so ill advised that she intended to rely on a soothsayer for guidance.

"Begging your pardon, milord, but are we qualified to judge?" Rodgers asked. "It has been my observation that we English tend to look askance at whatever we are unable to explain."

"Your mind, Rodgers, would appear to be so open to exotic notions that all manner of rubbish has entered and accumulated there." Clasping his hands behind him, Devon paced to and fro. "This is not the time for philosophy but for deeds." He lowered his head and, continuing to pace, muttered to himself as he sought to hit upon a suitable course of action. Finally he stopped dead, faced Rodgers and exclaimed, "Of course, the eclipse! I should have remembered the eclipse as soon as you spoke of an astrologer."

"The eclipse, milord?"

"The almanac reports that there will be a partial eclipse of the moon in a fortnight's time."

"Caused, I believe, by our planet Earth passing between the sun and the moon."

"Is there anything in heaven or on earth you stand in ignorance of, Rodgers?"

"Many things, including the use you mean to make of this forthcoming eclipse. I should be greatly obliged if you would tell me."

"This eclipse of the moon provides an excellent excuse for an eclipse party, a rollicking ramble into the country for a few weeks, let us say to Mr. Gerard Kinsdale's estate where, far from the smoke of London, Round Hill will afford a panoramic view of the heavens."

"And I presume you, milord, are a friend of this Mr. Kinsdale."

"An acquaintance, yes, as was your employer, Mrs. Baldwin, in bygone days, in better days. Mr. Kinsdale, who has become something of a misanthrope in late years, is best known as an inventor, not of steam engines or large pieces of textile machinery, but of gadgetry. Recently, for example, he devised a shade for candles, a device akin to a lamp shade, a clever though rather impractical contrivance."

Rodgers looked thoughtful. "I believe Mrs. Baldwin has mentioned Mr. Kinsdale but I have, I must admit, never before heard of an eclipse party."

"Some five or six years ago, Lady Prescott held an extraordinarily successful eclipse party at Medford. One heard of little else for months thereafter."

"How strange. My brother happened to be in service with Lady Prescott at that time, as he is today, and never mentioned such an extraordinary event."

"Must you be so deucedly meticulous, Rodgers?

Whether the eclipse party occurred five years ago or ten and whether the hostess happened to be Lady Prescott or Lady Jersey or Lady Someone Else Entirely, makes little or no difference. The important thing is that you have now heard of an eclipse party given by a lady of quality; you are therefore now entitled to mention, when discussing the matter with Mrs. Baldwin, having heard of such a party. Do you take my meaning?"

Rodgers sighed. "I fear I do, milord."

"Think about the possibilities of an eclipse party if you will, Rodgers. Picture a company of ladies and gentlemen enjoying the balmy night air in the country while they cavort in the soft glow of the moonlight. What better setting could one imagine to further Miss Riggs's matrimonial prospects? As the poet said,

The moon shines bright:—in such a night as this . . .
Troilus methinks mounted the Troyan walls,
And sighed his soul toward the Grecian tents,
Where Cressid lay that night.

"Those wondrous lines are from William Shakespeare's *As You Like It.*"

"Much as it distresses me to contradict you, milord, methinks they appear in *The Merchant of Venice.*"

Devon's brow furrowed in thought as he glared at Rodgers. "Quite right," he admitted after a moment. He looked Rodgers up and down and suddenly grinned. "If ever you become dissatisfied with your present employment," he said, "pray make me aware of the fact for I shall most certainly have a place for you here."

Rodgers made a slight bow. "Thank you, my lord," he said, "but I am more than content where I am . . ."

Later, after Rodgers had left to deliver the letter to Mlle. Gauthier, Devon stared from the window, congratulating himself on his idea of an eclipse party. It would be just the thing.

On the other hand, Miss Riggs's consultation with an astrologer was less than satisfactory. He had a strong premonition, in fact, that endless mischief would flow from such an undertaking.

Five

Justine and Prudence Baldwin were greeted at the door by Antonio, Mlle. Gauthier's young footman. *"Mademoiselle* is expecting you," he told the two visitors in accented English.

He led them down a long carpeted corridor, their way dimly lit by candles in elaborately carved sconces placed below alabaster statues set in niches along both walls. As she looked more closely at the statues, Justine drew in her breath in sudden shocked surprise while at the same time, fascinated despite herself, she felt compelled, even as she felt her face glow with a vivid flush, to gaze more closely at the entwined bodies of men and women.

The life-sized figures represented classic Greek and Roman scenes of myth and legend, the men nude, the women either unclothed or revealingly clad in flowing diaphanous gowns, the soft light from the candles glowing on their white breasts and buttocks. To Justine's right, a conquering warrior carried off a desperately struggling woman into the horrors of depraved captivity; there, on the opposite wall, two lovers embraced, their bodies molded one to the other in never-ending, yet never-to-be-fulfilled passion.

Justine blinked as the corridor suddenly brightened. Looking away from the statues she realized that Antonio had opened a door and was announcing their arrival. Embarrassed at her dallying, she hurried forward to follow Prudence into a spacious room where her gaze was immediately drawn upward to the opaque glass ceiling decorated with the twelve signs of the zodiac, from Aries to Pisces, circling as they followed the path of the sun as seen from the Earth.

She breathed in a heady odor, the intoxicating scent of a spicy incense bringing to her mind exotic Eastern pleasure palaces ruled by sultans in turbans and long robes of varied colors where languorous white-skinned, black-eyed women reclined on oversized pillows as they idled their days away while awaiting—with apprehension? with indifference? with anticipation?—the words that would summon them to the chambers of their lord and master.

By the light of votive candles burning steadily in many-tiered candelabra, she saw that red and green velvet draperies had been drawn across the windows. The tapestries on the walls depicted strange, unsettling scenes: sacrificial virgins mounting the stone steps of an ancient New World temple, Satan in the form of a snake with a man's head enticing Adam and Eve in the Garden of Eden, dancing druids circling a huge oak in a medieval English forest, the abduction and rape of the Sabine women, and "Mars and Venus United in Love."

Prudence, seemingly oblivious to the sensuousness of her surroundings, hurried across the room to give a most cordial greeting to the woman rising from her chaise longue. Turning to Justine, she said with obvious pride, "This is Daphne Gauthier."

Mlle. Gauthier, a petite blue-eyed woman of a certain age, had curly hair whose ash blondness, Justine could not fail to observe, owed more to artifice than to nature, just as her vivid cheeks gave evidence rather of a liberal use of rouge than of robust health.

"Do sit beside me," Mlle. Gauthier purred. When Justine joined her on the chaise longue, Mlle. Gauthier took her right hand and studied it intently. The three women were silent as the reader traced the lines on Justine's palm with the tip of her finger. "This palm shows the outer person," she said, "the left palm reveals the inner." When she had finished studying both of Justine's hands she said, "Exactly as I suspected."

Prudence leaned forward eagerly. "What do you see, Daphne?" she asked. "Tell me, I beseech you."

"Justine—even though we have never met before, I feel I know you so well already that I must take the liberty of calling you by your given name—I see you as a bright, lively young lady of great hidden warmth, of sudden violent enthusiasms, one who shows affection readily, perhaps too readily since you constantly risk disappointment." Mlle. Gauthier paused as though seeking confirmation of her reading, but Justine said nothing.

"You tend to be impatient with those who are slow to make up their minds," Mlle. Gauthier went on. "You crave more challenge than is offered by the normal domestic duties of a woman, a craving which, in our day and age, may very well lead you to suffer much unhappiness and frustration."

From the corner of her eye, Justine noted that Prudence was nodding in agreement and smiling as if more than satisfied by this display of Mlle. Gauthier's talents. Justine herself could not quarrel with Mlle. Gauthier's description of her personal traits.

"When I look into your past," Mlle. Gauthier went on, "I perceive a time of great happiness when you were very young." She frowned. "This happiness, unfortunately, was followed by a terrible tragedy when you were a girl of eight or nine—" She stopped when Justine caught her breath in surprise, then, taking her hand once more, said, "Notice this interruption in your life line."

There was, Justine saw, a decided break in the line on her palm.

"This tragedy," Mlle. Gauthier said, "caused you many years of sorrow and distress. And now, though for the most part recovered from your loss, you are fated to face a year of uncertainty, a year of great danger and yet one of extraordinary opportunity."

"How remarkable," Prudence said.

There was nothing at all remarkable in any of this, Justine assured herself while denying that she was in any way shaken by the accuracy of Mlle. Gauthier's revelations. The soothsayer could easily have discovered a great deal about her by merely asking a few questions. Prudence, in fact, could have told her of Justine's past without realizing how much she was revealing.

"I suspect," Mlle. Gauthier said, "that our young

friend fails to find my reading of her palm at all remarkable."

Justine felt herself blushing. "The future," she said, "are you able to tell me what my future holds other than the uncertainty we all face?"

"Especially," Prudence put in, "with regard to possible affairs of the heart. Though she has never said as much, I presume that Justine, like all unattached young ladies, must often tire of her state of single blessedness."

"For mere mortals such as ourselves," Mlle. Gauthier said softly, "the future is always hidden behind a veil. Even when the veil lifts for a moment, we see through a glass darkly. There are so many possible paths one may follow, so many unexpected twists and turnings along the way."

"You must make the attempt," Prudence said. "I so rely on your guidance in making plans for Justine."

"For you, my dear friend, I shall do my best." Mlle. Gauthier closed her eyes, raising her head heavenward. "Ah," she said after a few moments, her eyes still closed, "I do see a man, a man of pleasing countenance, a gentleman held in high regard by the *ton*."

"Wonderful!" Prudence cried. "And does he possess feelings of tenderness for Justine?"

"I could tell you more if only I were better acquainted with both Justine and the gentleman. He shows an interest in Justine, of that I am confident, an interest that may one day, possibly soon, blossom into true affection. And yet there are obstacles in the path of this romantic attachment, many obstacles, not the least of which is a disparity in social standing."

Justine could do nothing to still the rapid beating

of her heart since Mlle. Gauthier could be describing only one person. Was it possible he did care for her? She sighed. Of course not—Mlle. Gauthier meant to dangle tempting possibilities before Prudence and herself; the soothsayer was no more able to see into the future than she, Justine, was.

Mlle. Gauthier opened her eyes to peer closely at Justine. "Another obstacle is your own nature, my dear," she said. "An Aries such as yourself is apt to love most unwisely, an Aries tends to love with a strong, fiery passion, a passion that consumes all in its path and leaves you with nothing but cold ashes."

"You must tell us who this mysterious gentleman is," Prudence begged. "You have me all in a dither." She put her hand to her breast. "My poor heart!"

My poor heart, Justine echoed to herself. Was she indeed to be left with nothing more than ashes? Not if she could prevent such an unhappy fate! And yet, if he *did* care for her . . .

Mlle. Gauthier smiled. "He is," she said, her voice rising in an excited spiral as she spoke, "a gentleman of the *ton,* a handsome young man that many mothers have dangled for to no avail. Are you unable to guess?"

Both Justine and Prudence shook their heads.

"He is," Mlle. Gauthier said, raising both hands triumphantly, "none other than Mr. John Willoughby!"

With a light Chinese shawl over her nightgown, Justine opened the French doors of her bedchamber and stepped out onto the room's small balcony. The night seemed even hotter than the day had been, the air heavy and suffocating. Clouds huddled low over the city while in the east lightning flickered just above the horizon, but no breeze came to stir the drooping branches of the weeping willow in the garden.

"John Willoughby." Justine shook her head as she murmured the name since she considered her distant cousin, as she had told Prudence on their drive home from Mlle. Gauthier's, a pleasant young man who seemed to better fill the role of a brother rather than a lover.

"Time not only mends the worst of wounds," Prudence had replied, "but often illuminates the shadowed recesses of our hearts as well, revealing love where once only friendship dwelled. We must be patient, we must wait and see what the excursion to the country for the eclipse party brings."

An eclipse party; what an unusual yet delightfully appealing notion. And to think that Rodgers had suggested the idea; an extremely clever man, Rodgers, a true paragon. She quite enjoyed their frequent conversations. If Gerard Kinsdale consented to act as their host for a stay of a few weeks in the country (and Prudence seemed certain he would consent), John Willoughby would be present, of course. Prudence also intended to invite John's sister, his uncle, and Lord Alton, as well as several other gentlemen and ladies.

But what of Lord Devon? Justine sighed; his name had not been mentioned.

Leaving the doors to the balcony open in the hope of encouraging at least the hint of a breeze, Justine returned to her chamber, removed her shawl and drew the coverlet off the four-poster bed. She lay on her back on the sheet and closed her eyes.

When thoughts and images insisted on roiling in her mind, she pictured, as she often did to hasten sleep, the vast vault of the limitless and silent heavens, the clusters of sun-stars whirling through space, the planets orbiting our sun, the moons circling the planets . . .

Clothed in a long flowing silk dressing gown and nothing more, she was led by two men, looming dark shadows in the gloom, down a long dank corridor with water dripping from overhead. No, not a corridor, the harsh damp rock beneath her bare feet told her she was in a cavern far beneath the earth. A light glinted ahead of her and, as she neared the candle flame she saw a statue of lovers, both unclothed, in a niche in the cave wall.

As she passed the niche she gasped, looking back over her shoulder to stare in horrified fascination. Surely the man had moved. Yes, he had, even now his hand was sliding along the smooth curve of the woman's back. They were not plaster, not marble, but alive, as surely flesh and blood as she herself.

A hand gripped her arm, hurrying her on and the two lovers were swallowed by the darkness of the cave.

Another light appeared ahead of her and she saw that she was approaching another niche. At first she looked steadfastly away but then, in spite of herself, she glanced into the niche. This *was* a statue, she thought with a relieved sigh, a depiction of two men holding a struggling, naked woman aloft between them.

As Justine looked away, she heard a woman scream.

She turned and saw, before she was forced onward, her pulses racing, the naked woman screaming in terror as she was borne to the ground.

Glaring sunlight blinded her. Squinting into the light, she realized that a door had been opened just ahead of her. When her vision cleared, she stared up at massive stone steps rising into a bright blue sky. Her two captors gripped her arms, forcing her to mount the steps between them, the stone cloyingly wet under her feet from, she thought at first, water, but when she glanced down she saw what she had imagined to be water was in fact the dull red of partially congealed blood. Her senses reeled.

She was half-prodded, half-carried to the vast flat top of the pyramid. A darkly stained stone block reared precisely in the center of the expanse. She cringed away in fear; however she was led not to the block but to a curtained enclosure at the edge of the pyramid. One of her captors threw back the curtain to reveal a tall, imposing man standing within, whose arms were folded over his chest. He was dressed in a robe of scarlet and orange, wore a circular headdress concealing his hair and a grotesque black mask covering his face. Justine knew without being told that he was the high priest.

Her two captors led her to the priest, stopping abruptly when they were an arm's length away. At a signal from the priest, they forced her to her knees in front of him. Slowly the priest raised his hands and started to lift the mask from his face . . .

She woke and sat up in bed, her body damp with perspiration, eerily unsettled by her dream while at the same time aware of being awakened by a harsh sound without being certain what had caused it. Leaving her bed, she walked through the door onto the balcony. Lightning flashed above the chimney pots; a rumble of thunder followed almost immediately. Had thunder wakened her, or had it been a sound close to the house, in the street, perhaps, or closer still, in the garden, or—and she glanced about her apprehensively at the thought—in the house itself?

Justine peered into the darkness of the garden below her, seeing nothing, hearing nothing. Evidently, she assured herself with a sigh of relief, the sound had been either the thunder or a phantom sound from her dream.

After she returned to her bed, fragments of her disquieting dream came back, causing her to shake her head as if by doing so she could banish the feverish memories of desire and danger. But to no avail for the dream images remained to haunt her as she turned from side to side seeking sleep.

A noise startled her, a sound coming from her chamber, the sound of stealthy movement. She shivered with apprehension. Something, no, not something, someone, an intruder, must be in the room with her. Lightning flashed nearby; she saw a figure silhouetted in the darkness, the figure of a man crouched at the foot of her bed. She opened her mouth to scream but no sound came, she was frozen with fear, totally unable to move or to cry out.

The intruder drew nearer, now he was at the side of her bed, now he knelt on the edge of the bed itself. His hand reached toward her cringing body, his fingers touched the flesh of her bare arm. She screamed.

And came awake to a vivid flash. A thunderous

roar reverberated through the room. She stared about her in confusion. Again lightning flashed, revealing an empty chamber, again thunder rumbled, and she realized with a surge of relief she had dreamed not once but twice.

With a hissing rush, the rain began, a heavy rain that drummed on the roof. Justine swung from her bed and when, in the flicker of the lightning, she saw the rain slant beneath the balcony roof and into her room, she hurried to the French doors, intending to close them, only to pause when a wave of cool, invigorating air swept over her.

After a moment of hesitation, she left the doors open and stepped out onto the balcony into the long-awaited rain, the cooling, cleansing, life-giving rain. She raised her arms, lifted her head toward the sky, feeling the insistent beat of the rain as the water soaked her hair, streamed down her cheeks and molded her thin gown to her body.

"Yes," she murmured, welcoming the rain and the change in the weather. "Yes, yes," she said aloud, anticipating the adventure of her new life in London, embracing life and all it offered. "Yes, yes, yes."

Six

"Years ago," Prudence said as their carriage left the high road and started the last leg of their journey to Gerard Kinsdale's estate, "we always caught our first glimpse of the chimneys of Kinsdale Manor from here. Now you can see nothing but the trees."

"Did you visit the Manor often when you were young?" Justine asked.

"On many, many occasions. Oh, I shall never forget the routs, the balls, the gay parties, all the wonderful times we had." Prudence closed her eyes as she recalled those long-ago days. "How very handsome Gerard was, how extraordinarily charming, how inconstant. I think we all must have been in love with him at one time or another, and he with us; I know I was, or thought I was until I met Eustace. Gerard loved all of us, one this week, another the next, while Eustace loved only me."

"How sad that Mr. Kinsdale never married."

"Oh, but he did, I thought you knew he married. His bride was Fanny Ryder, *the* Fanny Ryder, one of Mr. Romney's favorite subjects. He must have painted her portrait five times or more. When she passed on to a better world after being married less than a year (the Ryders have always been notorious for their weak lungs), Gerard abandoned London to live in the country. We all expected him to return to town after his year of mourning ended but he never did. I suspect he mourns poor Fanny even after all these many years."

Prudence shook her head as if to admonish herself. "We should be looking forward to the eclipse party and your opportunity to become better acquainted with Mr. John Willoughby, rather than reminiscing." She nodded to her right. "Those are the Manor gates, the house is almost a mile further on." She pursed her lips in disapproval. "How ill kept the grounds are."

Glimpsing sunlight sparkling from the waters of a stream, Justine drew in an uneasy breath, disquieted but unsure of the reason. And then she remembered. Closing her eyes, picturing a rowboat, she was whisked back to her childhood.

She had been seven when, though forbidden by her father to brave the river alone, she had pushed the rowboat from the muddy bank and clambered aboard. Struggling with the heavy oars, she made little progress at first but then was drawn farther and farther from shore by the inexorable current. Too proud to cry out for help, she watched in helpless terror as the small boat was swept toward the falls.

Somehow, though fear blurred the details, her father had rescued her.

Now, as they drove along the approach to the Manor, she felt the disquieting sensation of again being swept away from the safety of the shore toward the unknown. And she no longer had a father to save her.

As they entered the park, three mongrel dogs ran from the trees to yap at the horses' hooves, retreating at the flick of Rodgers's whip but returning to run beside one of the rear wheels, barking incessantly. Only when Rodgers guided the carriage into the sweep leading to the mansion did the dogs draw back, still barking, and then reluctantly lope away to disappear amidst the trees.

"How sad," Prudence murmured.

For a moment Justine thought she referred to the stray dogs, but she quickly saw that her friend's gaze was on the topiary garden in the center of the sweep. The garden's shrubs, once meticulously fashioned in the form of birds and animals, had been allowed to sprout in unpruned abandon until they were now only vaguely recognizable.

Sad? Justine could not agree with Prudence and so she said nothing. In fact, she felt a certain kinship with the shrubs since in the last few weeks she had found herself being pruned and trimmed to change her into a different person, one she had difficulty recognizing as Justine Riggs. Those exuberantly sprouting shrubs might not please the eye, but at least they more closely resembled Nature's intention of what a shrub should be.

"My heart aches," Prudence said, "to find the mansion in such a sorry state of disrepair."

Justine noted that bricks had fallen from the chimneys, slates were missing from the roof, and the ivy climbing the walls had spread unchecked until the leafy vines covered many of the windows.

"The Manor," Prudence went on with a sigh, "reminds me of an old, old man grown too tired or too forgetful to care about his appearance. I wonder if Gerard—" She shook her head and sighed once more.

When their carriage stopped beneath the porte cochère, Justine noticed that weeds had invaded the cracks between the stones of the steps leading to the entrance. When no one came from the house to meet them, Rodgers sent a footman scurrying to the bell pull beside the front door while he swung to the ground to help Prudence and Justine alight from the carriage.

After an inordinately long wait, the door was opened by an aged servant in old-fashioned, wrinkled livery. Blinking in the sunlight—the entryway behind him, dark and musty, reminded Justine of a cavern—he mumbled words they were unable to understand. Turning, he led Prudence and Justine, unsteady step by unsteady step, slouching through the gloom to a candlelit drawing-room where a tall, exceedingly thin elderly gentleman hurried forward to greet them.

"My dear, dear Prudence!" Gerard Kinsdale cried, bowing stiffly and smiling crookedly, as though his social graces had grown rusty from lack of use. "After all these years," he told her, "I find you every bit as lovely as on the day we met."

"Nor have you changed, Gerard," Prudence said softly.

If Prudence was referring to his garb, Justine told herself, she was most certainly being faithful to the truth, since Gerard Kinsdale wore what she suspected had been the height of fashion forty years before: shoes fastened by enormous silver buckles, white stockings with their tops tucked beneath blue breeches, a knee-length coat of a darker shade of blue adorned with oversized white buttons and, as his crowning splendor, a powdered wig.

After greeting Justine, Gerard proceeded to fuss over Prudence, holding a chair for her, offering her refreshments, inquiring after her comfort and the state of her health. Justine had heard of gentlemen dancing attendance on ladies but had never witnessed the phenomenon before. Was it possible, she wondered, that her rather acerbic reaction resulted from envy? No one had ever treated her in such a solicitous manner.

Gerard's rapt gaze, she noted, never left Prudence's face nor did his attention flag for as long as an instant while he listened to a lengthy catalog of her latest ailments. In fact, he nodded with obvious concern at the mention of each and every symptom.

"Are we the first guests to arrive?" Justine asked, during a lull in the litany of maladies.

"You are," Gerard said, "and you deserve an explanation as to why I invited Prudence and yourself for today and the others for tomorrow." He nodded toward Prudence. "I must beg you to assist me," he said. "By now you realize that the Manor and its staff are not what they were in those wonderful days of our youth. When your eminent young gentleman friend requested me to host this party, I declined with great vehemence—until I learned that you, my dear Prudence, would be among the guests."

Eminent young gentleman friend? Justine repeated to herself. She had been under the impression that Prudence, with Rodgers's assistance, had made the arrangements for the eclipse party. Was it possible that Gerard was referring to Lord Devon? she wondered with a flutter of hope. If it had been Lord Devon, why had he seen fit to involve himself?

"Will you help me, Prudence?" Gerard pleaded. "You and Miss Riggs? I have not the slightest notion as to what pleases the ladies and gentlemen of the *ton* these days; I long ago turned my back on the frivolity of society. I will do everything in my power to assist you, now and always, as will each and every member of my staff, though I fear we have all grown old together. Will you, Prudence?"

Prudence raised her hand to her bosom; her breathing quickened. "I feel quite faint," she gasped.

Gerard stared in surprise before kneeling at her side, wincing when he was forced to bend his knees. He took her hand in his, at the same time glancing over his shoulder in search of help. Justine, accustomed by now to Prudence's spells, calmly removed the vinaigrette containing smelling salts from her reticule and wafted it back and forth under Prudence's nose.

Prudence blinked. "Whatever happened?" she asked.

"Mr. Kinsdale asked for our help in planning the eclipse party," Justine said briskly. "We should help him; in fact it appears we must help him if the party is to be anything other than a dismal failure."

"I know absolutely nothing of eclipse parties," Prudence said helplessly.

"The guests arrive tomorrow?" Justine asked, when it became obvious she would have to fill the breach.

Gerard nodded.

Justine frowned in thought. "And the eclipse is the

84

day after, a few minutes before midnight. We can best view it from a nearby hill?"

"South Hill is less than a mile from the Manor."

Justine nodded. "Tomorrow we might have an informal excursion of some sort, a picnic perhaps; yes, I believe a picnic in a glade in the park would be delightful if we have more of this wonderful weather, with outdoor games for both the gentlemen and ladies to follow. Archery? Is an archery contest possible? And on the day of the eclipse we should have a formal dinner in the evening followed by dancing—there must surely be a large enough room in the Manor for dancing—and after the dancing we must all drive to South Hill to view the eclipse. Or perhaps the dancing should take place on our return."

Immediately after Justine began to make her suggestions, Gerard began shaking his head. As soon as she finished he raised his hands in a helpless gesture. "Quite impossible," he said regretfully. "What you suggest would require at least a week of preparation."

"In that event," Justine said, "we must devise a simpler program."

"I refuse to hear of any changes." Prudence seized command, apparently completely recovered from her attack of the vapors. "We must do every last thing you proposed, Justine. I see you shaking your head, Gerard, but it *is* possible."

"And yet," Justine said, "I have not the slightest notion where or how to begin."

"Being of a certain age, as I am," Prudence declared, "does offer compensations. It gives me the benefit of many years of experience in solving similar dilemmas."

Justine must have showed her skepticism for Prudence went on, "Yes, I have surmounted even more difficult obstacles, I most certainly have. Not in the giving of parties or the arranging of balls or the holding of dinners, perhaps, but in accomplishing what at first blush seemed altogether impossibly difficult."

"If you say all this is feasible, my dear Prudence," Gerard said, "it is as good as accomplished. How you shall work this miracle, I do not know, but I have every confidence in you."

"How kind you are, Gerard."

They seemed, Justine thought, more interested in one another than in making plans for the entertainment of Gerard's guests. Though she felt pleased that they took such pleasure in each other's company, it did not bode well for the party.

"If you would summon Rodgers," Prudence said, "we will begin our preparations."

When Rodgers came to her, Prudence described the activities suggested by Justine and related Gerard's offer to make his servants available to help with any and all of the necessary work. "Do you understand what we require, Rodgers?" she asked.

"Perfectly, madam, your explanation is eminently clear. As always."

"Excellent. I shall therefore leave the matter entirely in your capable hands.",

With a slight though deferential bow, Rodgers left the room.

Gerard looked from the empty doorway to Prudence. "And this Rodgers of yours will perform the required miracle?" he asked. When she nodded, he shook his head in wonderment.

So this was the way the gentry were able to survive and prosper, Justine told herself. At this moment, throughout the length and breadth of England, counterparts of Rodgers were assuring the smooth functioning of the town houses of the wealthy, managing their country estates and overseeing their vast landholdings. It was a stratagem she must always have vaguely suspected; it was a truth she would remember.

Justine came from her reverie to hear Gerard urging Prudence and herself to join him in an hour's time for an early "country" dinner. "Afterwards, my dear Prudence," he said, with the hesitancy of a shy young man asking the belle of the ball to favor him with a dance, "I have a surprise for you. And for you as well, Miss Riggs."

When they finished eating, Gerard eagerly escorted his two guests to the library where he seated them in front of a table holding three objects covered with green velvet cloths. Carefully lifting the first of the cloths, he said with pride, "Behold."

Puzzled, Justine stared at a candleholder containing a tall yellow candle whose exposed wick was shielded by a green shade.

"This," Gerard told them with a mixture of pride and diffidence, "is one of my latest inventions, a candle shade. As you see, the shade is attached to the candle by this metal loop so as the candle burns and melts the shade lowers itself."

"How ingenious!" Prudence exclaimed. "I never would have believed it possible."

Gerard smiled. "What other men view as difficulties, I see as opportunities," he said as he stepped to one side so he stood behind the second cloaked object.

"Here," he told them as he whisked away the cloth to reveal a rounded metal post whose top had been painted a bright orange, "is my model of an improved bollard. You both have undoubtedly seen the black bollards placed at the four corners of the intersections of busy London streets to prevent carriages from mounting the walkways. *My* bollard is distinctive because of its color. My experiments have demonstrated that this particular shade of orange is much more visible than the black which is customarily used."

"Wonderful," Prudence said. "Yours is a distinct improvement over any bollard I have ever seen."

"Thank you, my dear Prudence." He removed the cloth from the third and final display of the fruit of his creative imagination. "Miss Riggs," he said, "what would you say we have here?"

"A duck," she told him, pleasantly surprised by the decoy's lifelike appearance, "a blue-winged teal."

"Exactly," Gerard said, evidently surprised in turn by her knowledge of waterfowl. Taking a key from the pocket of his coat, he inserted it beneath the wing of the duck. "I have been toiling on this creation for the past six months," he said as he began turning the key, "and still the result is less than satisfactory."

Removing the key, Gerard stepped back from the table. The duck—constructed, Justine realized, of metal—emitted a whirring sound as both wings slowly rose and then fell, rose and then fell once more. The whirring continued as the duck lurched up onto its short legs, waddled toward them, hesitated, and, with a plaintive screech, collapsed sideways to lie unmoving on the table.

Prudence clapped her hands in appreciation; Justine

smiled uncertainly; Gerard shook his head ruefully. "Soon," he promised them, "I expect to create a mechanical duck so real in its behavior that no one will be able to decide whether it is alive or not."

"Have you attempted to sell any of your inventions?" Justine asked.

Gerard gave her a scornful look. "You would have me enter the marketplace?" he asked. "You suggest that a gentleman should engage in trade? Certainly not. I invent for my own amusement, not for the enrichment of some merchant."

"Quite right," Prudence said. "Oh, Gerard," she sighed, "I only wish I possessed but one-fifth of your genius."

Gerard beamed with pleasure . . .

Much later, as Justine and Prudence climbed the curving stairway to their chambers, Justine said, "I admit Gerard is clever but his inventions *are* rather impractical, are they not?"

"Of course they are," Prudence agreed. "As a young man, Gerard was always impractical. Fortunately for him, he entered his more mature years without what my mother always described as the greatest burden an elderly man or woman can be forced to carry."

"And that is?"

"An empty purse. Gerard's purse has always been full to overflowing."

Justine smiled and nodded.

"I gather," Prudence went on, "you considered my praise for his inventions overly enthusiastic."

"A wee bit," Justine admitted.

Prudence paused at the top of the stairs. "If I have

learned anything at all in my sixty-three years, it is that we women must always remember one important fact: men are like children and we should treat them as such. They thrive on praise, the more extravagant the better; rebukes of any sort tend to destroy what little self-confidence they possess. When a man asks me for my opinion about some supposedly marvelous feat of his, he seeks my favorable opinion. To give him my honest opinion would be decidedly bad form."

Justine considered her friend's words. "Yet men must recognize insincerity when they hear it," she protested mildly.

"Oh me, oh my, how blissfully ignorant of life you seem at times. As I said, men are akin to children. When we entertain children with tales of fairies and elves and Saint Nicholas, they may very well realize that these are mere fables, yet they bring themselves to believe us because they have such a monstrous need to believe. Men will accept as sincere whatever confirms their high opinion of themselves."

"But surely not all men are so vain."

"No, not all. If you gathered one hundred gentlemen at random, perhaps the rule would apply to only ninety-six or ninety-seven." Prudence started toward her bedchamber only to hesitate. "No matter how much it goes against your grain," she counseled, "you must school yourself to defer to men. If you wish to avoid awkward situations, you must learn to listen to their notions, no matter how hare-brained they may be, and agree with them. Most importantly, Justine, you must never again challenge a man as you did by racing Lord Devon in the park."

The memory of the race still had the power to cause Justine to sigh ruefully. Not because she had accepted the challenge but because she had neglected to question her mount's pedigree.

"But I wonder," she said thoughtfully, "if I could ever respect such a man as you describe."

"You have the habit, Justine, of butting me too many buts. The alternative to following my suggestions is plain—you will be doomed to the life of a spinster." Prudence nodded emphatically, bade Justine good-night, and walked away along the corridor only to look back when she reached the door to her bedchamber. "And," she said, "if you believe Lord Devon is an exception to what I say, you are fated to suffer a rude awakening."

Before Justine could collect enough of her wits to reply, Prudence shut the door of her bedchamber.

The guests began arriving late the following morning and, shortly before five in the afternoon, the party set off in a caravan of carriages to picnic in the park a short distance from the Manor.

On arriving at the glade, they found Rodgers and the Kinsdale servants standing guard over food and wine tastefully arranged on Holland cloths spread over the grass. The young people sat on folded blankets, the older guests, as well as the fastidious Lord Alton, on chairs. Justine, seated beside John Willoughby and half listening to his amiable prattle, denied to herself that she was sorely disappointed by Lord Devon's failure to attend the eclipse party. She was, or so she told herself, content to listen to John—

who was, after all, quite charming in his way—as she watched the other guests.

Lord Alton, bored and unhappy, took every possible occasion to declare all picnics uncivilized abominations, and sat by himself, from time to time raising his quizzing glass to stare balefully at anyone courageous enough to address a remark to him.

Their host, the bewigged and perspiring Gerard Kinsdale, hurried about fetching choice morsels to tempt Prudence's appetite. To Justine's surprise, she had yet to hear Prudence complain about the danger to her health posed by this excursion into the wilderness.

Stewart Ogden was regaling an unenthusiastic cluster of young people with a rambling anecdote about his walking tour in the Lake Country in the nineties. Emeline, sitting at his side, nodded and smiled as she listened but Justine had the impression she had heard the story many times before. Emeline had a kind heart, much kinder than her own. Justine set herself the goal of emulating her friend.

Mlle. Gauthier, garbed in a flowing red and green gypsy costume, was telling the fortune of a Miss Violet Holme, an amiable though shy young lady whose father, an admiral, happened to be a distant relative of the Willoughbys. Justine hoped she and Violet might have the chance to become better acquainted.

As they finished eating, Rodgers approached Prudence and whispered in her ear. Prudence, in turn, spoke a few words to Gerard who stood, raised one hand aloft and cleared his throat several times to ask for quiet.

"The targets for the archery competition," he announced, "are in place in the east meadow."

As the guests walked along a shaded path on their way to the meadow, Prudence left Gerard's side to wait for Justine. "I hope you took what I told you yesterday to heart," she said. "You must do nothing to wound a man's pride. And," she added with emphasis, "Mr. Willoughby, I am informed, considers himself an excellent marksman with bow and arrow."

Justine nodded but all she said was, "I remember your advice, Prudence."

Arriving at the site of the contest, they found two targets, each with five alternating white and black concentric circles, placed in the meadow some fifty paces distant. After consulting briefly with Rodgers, Gerard announced, "Each archer will be permitted two practice shots followed by six shots for score."

Eight of the guests had entered the competition, three of the ladies and five of the men.

"The ladies have the honor of shooting first," Gerard told them. "Miss Willoughby?"

Emeline walked uncertainly to the post marking the shooting station, decided not to take any practice shots, nocked an arrow and drew her bow. Her arrows waffled erratically on their way to the target, first to the right and then to the left.

"Two hits," Gerard declared after she shot her last arrow, "for twelve points." A hit in the center circle counted 9, the others 7, 5, 3, and 1, a scoring system introduced by the Prince Regent, a devotee of the sport, many years before when he was the Prince of Wales.

Justine followed Emeline. Her father had taught her

to use a bow and arrow but two years had passed since she had practiced and the bow felt heavy and awkward in her hands.

She sighted at the crotch of a tree far beyond the target, knowing her arrow would arc downward on its long flight, and she released her first practice arrow, watching it fly high and to the right. Resighting lower on the same tree, she shot again and saw her arrow strike the top of the target's outer circle.

She decided that if John Willoughby was an expert archer, as Prudence had said he was, he had little to fear from her. No harm would ensue, therefore, if she did her best. Making slight adjustments before each shot, she released her six arrows in rapid succession.

"Excellent," Gerard said, "the young lady has four hits for a total of twenty-two points."

There was a scattering of applause for her performance.

When John Willoughby's turn came—he shot last of all the eight archers—Justine's score was still high. John disdained taking any practice shots, releasing his arrows even more rapidly than Justine had. As soon as his sixth arrow struck the target, Gerard announced, "Six hits for twenty-two points. The match is even."

John Willoughby, Justine noted, glowered when he heard the result.

"I suggest that the contestants shoot alternately," Stewart Ogden said, "with each being given three shots to determine the winner."

"Agreed?" Gerard asked.

John frowned but agreed; Justine nodded, feeling somewhat uncomfortable.

She noticed Prudence looking at her in a speaking

way, her stern expression saying, "No matter what happens, Justine, you must not win."

"Miss Riggs will have the choice of whether to shoot first or second," Gerard said.

Justine hesitated. "Second," she decided as Prudence nodded her approval. By taking the last shot, she would be certain of John's score and so know how many points she needed to defeat him. Or, more importantly, the score that would fail to defeat him.

John Willoughby walked slowly forward, his complacency gone. He carefully drew his bow, aimed and released. A seven.

Justine nocked her arrow, raised and drew her bow, took careful aim. The arrow sped true. A nine! She heard a gasp of surprise from the spectators. John shot. Another seven. Again Justine aimed, shot, the arrow fluttering slightly, landing low. A three for a total of twelve. John's final arrow landed slightly high for a five, making his total nineteen.

Taking her last arrow, she raised the bow, hesitated, knowing she needed a seven to tie and a nine to win. How easy to miss slightly, how easy to lose honorably. She came to a decision and released her arrow, holding her breath as it whirred through the air on a long arc to the target where it thudded into the straw.

"By Jove!" Gerard cried. "A nine. Miss Riggs is the winner."

John Willoughby walked to her and bowed, offering his congratulations. How chagrined he seemed! She caught a glimpse of Prudence frowning and turning away.

There was a stir among the guests gathered near the path to watch and she turned, gasping when she saw Lord Devon stride from beneath the trees. "Since I was not present for the beginning of the competition," he said, "I claim the right to compete against the champion archer. Miss Riggs, do you accept my challenge?"

Seven

Gerard, frowning, glanced from Lord Devon to Justine. "Such a challenge is quite irregular," he said, obviously in a quandary as to how he should proceed.

"Perhaps irregular," Quentin said, "but surely not unheard of."

"What do *you* say, Miss Riggs?" Gerard asked. "Do you wish to accept Lord Devon's challenge or shall I declare the archery contest at an end?"

Justine noticed Prudence attempting to catch her eye while at the same time vigorously shaking her head as though she advised refusing the challenge or, if Justine did accept, telling her to be certain to lose.

Quentin, elegantly garbed in pale blue pantaloons, a waistcoat of a darker blue, and an intricately tied golden cravat, strode to Justine's side and murmured in a voice so low only she could hear, "Have no fear, Miss Riggs, I give you every assurance I shall allow you to win the competition."

Justine, who had been ready to agree to matching her skill at archery against Quentin's, tried unsuccessfully to suppress her anger. "Are you always so patronizing to women?" she whispered.

He raised one eyebrow. "My only intent was to behave as a gentleman should by deferring to a member of the weaker sex. You, my dear Miss Riggs, perceive slights where not only none are meant but none are given."

"Evidently your conception of how a gentleman should behave is far removed from mine." She added, mockingly, "Milord."

"God save us all." Quentin drew in an exasperated breath. "Then I take it you refuse my challenge?"

"I would accept on only one condition."

"And the condition is?"

"That you, my good Lord Devon, agree to offer yourself as my target."

Their gazes met, sparked, then held for a long moment as though the first to look away would be admitting defeat.

Quentin made a sweeping bow. "I readily accept your stipulation," he told her, a dare in his voice. Turning on his heel, he strode across the glade to the target where he swung about and faced her with his arms outstretched.

How arrogant he was, how sure of himself! She would not back down. Neither now nor ever. As she raised her bow, Justine heard murmurs of surprise and bewilderment from the guests. When she nocked an arrow the murmurs became gasps of alarm.

Slowly, Justine drew back the arrow and felt the bowstring grow taut. "Step aside, Lord Devon," she said, "you stand in harm's way."

Quentin merely smiled at her, a crooked smile that

mocked her, challenged her, dared her to carry out her threat. Could she hit the edge of the target, she wondered, without striking Quentin? Taking great care, she held her breath as she aimed.

A man's hand grasped her bow and jerked it upward. The arrow flew from her fingers to wing into the air, soaring higher and higher before slowing and, in a graceful arc, descending to bury itself in the ground halfway to the target.

"By God," Lord Alton told her, "I do admire your spirit." Keeping his grip on the bow, he eased it from her hand and tossed it to one side. "At times," he said with a meaningful glance at Quentin, "I must admit to having been sorely tempted to put a spoke in Quentin's wheel myself."

Realizing the eyes of all the guests were upon her, Justine made a valiant effort to convince them that she and Quentin had been play-acting. "I would never have harmed him,!" she said. "Or anyone else."

"Most certainly not," Lord Alton agreed, "at least not intentionally." His gaze lingered on her. "I must say I rather envy Devon for he has succeeded in attracting the attention of one of the most ravishing—" He broke off as Prudence Baldwin, her cane forgotten, hurried toward them. "I hope, Miss Riggs," he said, "that we will be able to continue this conversation at a more propitious time."

Justine nodded though she had scarcely heard him, much less understood what he was telling her. She started to glance toward Quentin when Prudence swept her away. "The carriages have arrived to take us to the Manor." Prudence lowered her voice. "You had no intention of actually shooting your arrow at Lord Devon, I trust."

This time Justine did look behind her and saw Quentin, surrounded by his friends, laughing as his pointing finger followed the course of an imaginary arrow that narrowly missed his left ear. She had expected him to be watching her, waiting to scornfully acknowledge her failure to carry out her threat, perhaps with a sardonic bow, perhaps with a mocking smile, but instead, she realized with a pang of disappointment, he was hurting her in the worst possible way: he was ignoring her.

Justine turned to Prudence. "Would I shoot Lord Devon?" she repeated. "Impale him with an arrow?" A glance at Quentin found him walking away from her. "I may have done so," she said, "and I may yet do so since he deserves no less!"

"Oh, my dear Justine." Prudence gave a mournful shake of her head. "Whatever shall I do with you?"

"I must be a terrible trial for you, dear Mrs. B. I do believe I should return to Gravesend where I belong."

Prudence gasped and then vigorously shook her head. The white-haired woman pressed a hand to her bosom, seeming to shrink into herself; a tear rolled down her cheek. "Whatever would I do without you?" she asked.

Justine, recalling that she had agreed to come to London to help Prudence, impulsively embraced the older woman. "I shall stay with you for as long as you can put up with my indiscreet ways," she promised.

"Then you shall stay forever." Prudence paused as

if to reconsider. "Or if not forever," she added, "at least until you are properly wooed and wed."

On their return to the Manor, Prudence retired to her sitting room and, as she was wont to do when faced with a disturbing and delicate situation, summoned Rodgers. She seldom directly asked him for suggestions, rather she offered a comment that was no more than a statement of fact, waited patiently and, sooner instead of later, he invariably offered his advice.

"The picnic," she began, "thanks to your efforts, proved an enormous success."

Rodgers accepted the compliment with a slight bow.

"In spite of the unfortunate incident during the archery contest," Prudence went on.

"Miss Riggs proved to be an excellent marksman. Or should I say markswoman?"

"I was referring to her contretemps with Lord Devon."

Rodgers smiled. "If only I had thought to provide apples as part of the picnic fare, Miss Riggs might have played the role of young William Tell. Or was it the father who shot the apple from his son's head?"

"Rodgers, I was not amused, I was decidedly not amused. Fearing the worst, I fully expected Justine to use Lord Devon as her target. My poor heart is still palpitating in a most irregular manner."

Rodgers inclined his head but said nothing.

"Tell me, Rodgers," Prudence went on, "what thoughts went through your mind when Justine threatened to let fly an arrow at Lord Devon?"

"You desire me to be completely truthful, madam?"

"Most certainly. You know how highly I value your candor."

"And you, madam, will treat my reply as confidential?"

"Rodgers, now you have me all aquiver with curiosity. You must tell me at once. I assure you whatever you may have thought at the time will go no further."

"When Miss Riggs raised her bow and took aim, I had a quite surprising and unexpected wish," Rodgers said. "No, not one wish, but two. I first wished myself younger by thirty or more years."

"I expect we all wish that at one time or another," Prudence said wistfully. "I often do."

"Not only did I wish to be younger but I also—" He hesitated. "But I also wished I occupied a higher station in life."

Prudence frowned as though the notion of a servant wishing to rise above himself was an alien concept. "I fail to see how your station in life pertains to Justine threatening Lord Devon."

"Miss Riggs displayed such panache, such spirit, such verve, that for a moment or two—no longer than that, I assure you—I wanted to be so situated in life, by both age and station, to be in a position that would allow me to offer for her hand."

Prudence stared at him, open-mouthed. "Rodgers," she said after a long pause, "you have no idea how shocked I am. You quite forget yourself."

"Quite right, madam, I deserve the severest of rebukes, but in my defense I must remind you I spoke only at your urging."

"Even so, you should have chosen to remain silent." Prudence shook her head. "Still, you have raised a possibility in my mind. Is it possible," she mused, "there might be gentlemen of the *ton* who would find her strange behavior appealing?"

"Indeed there might." When Prudence looked a question at him, he smiled slightly and said, "Lord Alton, for one, seemed rather taken with her."

"Lord Alton is a target quite out of our reach. Besides, I find him much too supercilious. More to the point is whether John Willoughby would find such unfeminine behavior appealing. I think not."

"I agree, madam. If I may be permitted to offer my personal observation, Mr. Willoughby has always seemed to be a most conventional young gentleman."

"And yet Daphne, Mlle. Gauthier, believes him to be the most likely suitor for Miss Riggs."

"Can it be, in this one instance at least, that Mlle. Gauthier is mistaken and Mr. Willoughby is not the best choice? Even the most perceptive and knowledgeable seers experience failure now and then. The signs and portents may be wonderfully precise, but they must always be interpreted by mere mortals."

Prudence nodded. "Daphne has admitted being fallible—and yet Mr. Willoughby is such an agreeable young man that I hate giving him up. I intend to consult with Daphne before we return to town so we can decide how to proceed. Ah, this is all so difficult, Rodgers. If only dear Eustace were here to help me."

"May I offer a suggestion, madam?" Although Rodgers spoke as though struck by a sudden inspiration, he covered his mouth with his hand to hide a small smile, a smile indicating, perhaps, that he had been waiting for this very opportunity. "Our host, Mr. Kinsdale," he said when Prudence nodded, "may be of some assistance to you as well since, in matters of this sort, a man's point of view is often of value."

"Gerard?" Prudence brightened. "The very thing. Thank you, Rodgers, I shall consult both Mlle. Gauthier and Gerard and the three of us will, I fervently hope, be able to set Justine's steps on the path leading to a suitable marriage."

The next evening, the evening of the eclipse of the moon, Gerard Kinsdale and his guests left the Manor shortly before nine for the short drive to Round Hill. As they jounced along a dirt track, Justine looked up from their open rig at the full moon rising above a haze on the horizon and at the stars just beginning to appear between clouds scudding eastward across the sky. She murmured a prayer that the clouds would disperse before the eclipse began.

Descending from the carriage at the foot of the hill with the ground mist eddying about her, Justine waved good-bye to Prudence who, with Daphne Gauthier, drove on along a circuitous road that would eventually take them to the summit of Round Hill. Justine and the other guests had elected to walk up the slope to the top.

Gerard Kinsdale joined her, and together they followed Rodgers, a lantern held aloft as he led the party along the path. Above them an irregular path of lights flared on the side of the hill where servants stood with torches to mark their way. At the summit a crown of torches ringed the massive domed rock that gave Round Hill its name.

They entered a woods, crossed a rushing stream on a log bridge, climbed slowly along a path zigzagging its way upward past an abandoned stone spring house and the rotting remains of a fence. When the trees thinned and the stars reappeared overhead, Rodgers stepped aside to wave them on toward the black dome of the summit.

Justine walked ahead of the others past baskets of food and wine, stepped between two torches embedded in the ground and then climbed the sloping rock to the very top of the hill where she stood breathing deeply of the balmy summer air as she looked below her where the light from the rising moon silvered the trees and glowed from the wraiths of white mist hovering above the fields. In the distance the lighted windows of the Manor blinked out one by one as the mist swirled higher.

She imagined herself alone, suspended between Earth and high heaven, on an island surrounded by a sea of white, an enchanted isle bathed in the soft glow of the moon, that lovely goddess of the night. The Earth, presently concealed by the mist, had always been a place of strife and discord, of wars and revolutions, of impoverished multitudes crowded into the dirty warrens of great cities. The heavens above her, on the other hand, were perfectly ordered, they were serene and chaste, pristine and beautiful. No wonder mankind had always sought answers to the mysteries of life on Earth by trying to solve the riddles of the stars and planets, of the sun and moon.

As she gazed up at the full moon, she imagined the

great pale orb slowly approaching the shadow of the Earth. She shivered. Soon the moon would be darkened. This, she realized, was not a portent of doom, was not a sign of the disfavor of the gods as the ancients had believed, and yet some primitive intimation of danger made Justine hug herself and look away from the heavens.

Seeing Prudence approaching on the arm of John Willoughby, Justine peered beyond them, past the circle of torches to where the figures of the arriving guests were silhouetted against the pale glow of the sky. Quentin was nowhere to be seen. How like him to frustrate her by shunning her after she had made up her mind to ignore him.

"What a terrible, terrible road," Prudence said as she and John came to stand beside her. "Being jolted unmercifully all the way up the hill made me come over queer. I do hope the eclipse will be worth the risk of the journey."

"How fortunate we are," John said, "to be granted a full moon on the night of the eclipse."

Justine started to speak but then, glancing at Prudence, held her tongue.

"The last time I saw an eclipse of the moon," Prudence said, "the moon was also full."

Justine bit her lip but found it impossible to remain silent any longer. "The moon," she said, "is always full during an eclipse since it must be on the opposite side of the Earth from the sun. Just as the moon is always new when it comes between the sun and Earth to make possible an eclipse of the sun."

"My word," John said, "you do have an impressive knowledge of the heavens." Shaking his head, he raised his spyglass for a better look at the panoply of stars. "I daresay I must have learned the names of the constellations years ago but I forgot them almost at once. How people are able to picture hunters and crabs and bears among the stars is bite beyond me."

"Someone once said," Justine told him, "that the creatures in the sky are characters in the oldest storybook in the world."

John gazed toward the north. "I can recognize the Little Dipper," he said.

"Ursa Minor."

"And the Big Dipper pointing to the North Star. I suppose it follows that the Big Dipper must be Ursa Major, the Great Bear."

Justine nodded and was about to name the major stars in the constellation when Prudence coughed and then cleared her throat. "I have such a scratchy throat after that interminable drive," she said, "and I do believe Rodgers brought some punch from the Manor. If you would be so kind, John—?"

"Of course," he said, "how thoughtless of me not to suggest it."

"Forgive me," Justine said after John hurried away. "At times I seem unable to hold my tongue when I realize I should. I know full well Mr. Willoughby has no desire to learn the proper names of the constellations or the phase of the moon during an eclipse."

"Ah, perhaps Mr. Willoughby does not," a nasal voice said, "but I do." A man's form materialized out of the darkness.

"Lord Alton," Justine said. "You do seem to have the knack of appearing from out of nowhere."

At that moment there was a sudden sigh from the

other watchers on the hill and, looking heavenward, Justine saw that the Earth's shadow had taken its first small bite from the side of the moon.

"The eclipse commences," Lord Alton announced as he bowed to Justine and Prudence. "When the dragon begins to devour the moon, disaster threatens. Or so I was told the ancients believed."

"Leading their medicine men to beat on drums, kettles, pans and gongs to frighten the dragon away."

Lord Alton smiled. "And since they were always successful in returning the moon to its original glory, they must have been hailed as saviors."

How very strange and confusing our sensibilities are, Justine thought as she nodded. While Lord Alton had never said or done the least thing to give her offense, she found his presence off-putting for he always succeeded in making her feel ill at ease. Quentin, on the other hand, seemed to delight in vexing her with behavior that was quite outside of enough, and yet, when not goaded to fury by his willful arrogance, she rather enjoyed his company.

"Extinguish the torches!" Rodgers called and, one by one, the fires were snuffed until the only light on the hilltop came from the soft silver glow of the moon and the stars.

"I believe, Mrs. Baldwin," Lord Alton told Prudence, "I just now observed Mr. Kinsdale searching for you but all in vain."

Prudence looked eagerly about her but then, her gaze returning to Lord Alton with a hint of suspicion in her eyes, she said rather tartly, "If so, I do believe he shall find me in time."

Lord Alton inclined his head to the older woman

before directing his attention to Justine. "I do happen to be acquainted with most of our northern constellations," he told her with a glance overhead, "—with the hunter in the sky, Orion, and with Cassiopeia, the lady in the chair, and my personal favorite, Draco, the dragon—perhaps the same dragon who at this moment is attempting to devour the moon."

"Either a dragon or a serpent," Justine put in.

"Around and around Polaris it circles, the dragon, or the serpent if you will, in pursuit of the fair maiden Cassiopeia. And all, alas, in vain."

"As the devil in the guise of a serpent pursued Eve in the Garden of Eden."

"Did Satan actually pursue Eve? I would say he was much too clever to pursue her; rather, he enticed her, he tricked her. And with much greater success than his heavenly counterpart has ever had."

"Are you saying, Lord Alton, that earth-bound women are more susceptible to the flattery and wiles of men than heavenly ones? Some of them may be, but, I assure you, not all are."

He smiled. "Including, I presume, yourself."

Before she could answer, John Willoughby, accompanied by his sister, appeared from the shadows carrying three glasses of punch. Lord Alton greeted the newcomers with a decided lack of enthusiasm and, directing a final unsettling glance at Justine, walked away.

As the moon slowly darkened, others came and went—Ogden Stewart, declaring the excursion to Round Hill to be a monstrous waste of time, Daphne Gauthier, all aflutter, and finally Gerard Kinsdale, offering a spate of apologies for having neglected Prudence for such an unconscionable length of time.

Gerard, with a promise of a better vantage point from which to view the climax of the eclipse, offered Prudence his arm. Justine started to follow them but, seeing them engrossed in one another, purposely lagged behind. When she looked above her she discovered that the moon was now completely darkened by the Earth's shadow.

"Miss Riggs."

At the sound of his voice she swung around, stifling a gasp.

"Have you ever considered," Quentin asked softly, "that these few moments, with the Earth wrapped in this unnatural darkness, might be a brief season of magic when our most unlikely dreams become possible? A precious time when we can set aside our normal humdrum selves? When we can behave on impulse without later having any regrets, without suffering any consequences?"

No, she told herself, she would not be seduced by his soft words. "And is this a time," she asked tartly, "when gentlemen such as yourself overindulge in the punch, Lord Devon?"

"Are you always sharp-tongued, Miss Riggs, even on such a special night as this? How can you be so mundane in the presence of this heavenly spectacle?"

"A total eclipse of the moon may be a relatively rare occurrence but it happens to be a perfectly natural phenomenon during which the shadow of the—"

"And the Big Dipper is properly called Ursa Major and the Little Dipper is properly known as—"

"You were eavesdropping!"

"Not at all. John Willoughby was kind enough to pass on your informative comments to me, undoubtedly in a vain attempt to educate me in some of the intricacies of astronomy." He paused. "Do you view every man you meet as a challenge of some sort? As someone you must defeat, whether by outracing him astride a steed or outshooting him in an archery contest or in a battle pitting your knowledge against his?"

How outrageous he was. Stung by the injustice of his accusations, she said, "I happen to be quite satisfied with the way I am and so I have no intention of trying to change. Not for John Willoughby or for you or for anyone else."

When he stepped toward her, a looming dark silhouette, his expression hidden by the darkness, her breath caught and her pulse raced. "If you—" she began but had to stop in a vain attempt to compose herself enough to keep her voice level. "If you find me so lacking in feminine traits," she asked, "why do you even bother wasting your valuable time trying to improve me?"

He sighed. "Because," he said, "for some reason I seem unable to help myself."

Reaching to her, he took her hand in his and started to raise her gloved palm to his lips. Justine snatched her hand away. She felt his hands close on her waist, his fingers almost circling her body. Even as she tugged at his wrists to push him away, he gathered her into his arms, his fingers sliding up her back to caress the nape of her neck. His lips brushed her cheek before closing over her mouth in a savage, demanding kiss.

Savoring the warmth of his embrace and the enticing sweetness of his lips, for a moment she surrendered herself to him and, despite herself, returned his kiss. And then, giving a strangled cry, she broke free and ran from him into the darkness.

Eight

On the following morning, Prudence, Daphne and Gerard entered the Manor drawing room only to find a Kinsdale maid standing on a chair using a piece of heavy cloth attached to a stick to swat at a cluster of flies on the panes of one of the long windows. A second maid waited below her to catch the dazed victims in a wide-mouthed glass jar. Other flies buzzed about the room.

"That fly-killer is one of my inventions," Gerard said proudly.

Prudence shook her head, drawing back in alarm, her hand clutching the lace neckline of her rose taffeta gown. "They do say flies carry disease," she said.

"Then we shall adjourn to the library." Gerard offered the two ladies his arms and they crossed the hall to the book room with its tier upon tier of volumes bound in vellum and tooled leather.

Once they were seated in a semicircle facing the fireplace, Prudence looked shyly from one to the other, hesitated, then plunged ahead. "I do so need your help," she said, going on to describe the dilemma created by Justine's hoydenish ways. "The poor thing suffered the misfortune of being raised not as a girl but as a boy," Prudence explained, "and now that she has reached a marriageable age her boyish ways are, to say the least, a problem. Rather than being attracted to her, gentlemen are put off."

"Lord Alton gave no evidence of being put off," Daphne objected. "In fact, he appeared quite intrigued by Justine's skill at archery. Not," she added hastily, "that I suggest him as a possible suitor. He is, after all, a member of the peerage."

"And, though I scarcely know the man," Gerard said, "I suspect he covets his single blessedness, and therefore whatever interest he may have in Miss Riggs has very little to do with matrimony."

Daphne sighed. "Unfortunately most men are so inclined. We members of the weaker sex must encourage them to realize the error of their ways by encouraging them to consider a more permanent arrangement."

Prudence shook her head. "I fear we digress. The question is who would be an appropriate suitor for Justine, rather than who would not."

"The stars told me," Daphne said, "that young John Willoughby would be ideal and, at first, he appeared rather enamored but after Justine bested him in the archery contest his interest, quite naturally, seemed to flag."

"I watched the two of them together," Gerard said, "and in my opinion the young lady offered Willoughby little encouragement. In fact, she offered him none at all. My view, of course, comes from someone who has been perched on a rather out-of-the-way shelf for many, many years and so you, Prudence, and you, Daphne, are much more qualified to judge these affairs of the heart."

Prudence shook her head. "Alas, the state of my health"—she glanced at Gerard and, as if regretting her hasty words, quickly added—"though recently much improved, has kept me from mingling in society."

"We require the assistance of someone who has been of the *ton,* a man of wide and varied acquaintance." Daphne suddenly brightened. "I know the perfect gentleman. Mr. Ogden Stewart."

"Young Willoughby's uncle?" Gerard shrugged. "Hardly know the man. Invited him here as a favor to Quentin. Are you acquainted with him, Prudence?"

"He has the reputation of being a misogynist, a gentleman who never married because he holds all women in disdain."

Daphne raised her eyebrows in surprise and then smiled, almost as though to herself. "I wonder if the truth of the matter might be somewhat different. Regardless, I suggest we invite him to help us if he will."

Again Gerard shrugged.

Prudence looked at Daphne in a questioning way before nodding and saying to Gerard, "Would you have one of the servants ask Ogden to come to us?"

When a scowling Ogden Stewart joined them, Prudence explained their predicament.

"You mean to tell me," Ogden blustered, "that you expect me to help you marry off that huntress, that young lady who wielded the bow and arrow? In my day we had none of this fuss and bother. In my day every young miss married the man her father selected for her without any ifs, ands, or buts."

Gerard shook his head. "I fear your memory fails you, sir. Most succeeded in marrying for what they deemed to be love."

"Love!" Ogden snorted. "Infatuation would be a better word to describe the emotion that afflicted them. Or a cruder term quite unfit for the ears of ladies."

"Mr. Stewart! Mind!" Prudence's unexpected sharpness caused the others to stare at her in surprise. As though equally startled by her own boldness, Prudence covered her mouth with her hand. "Justine has no mother and no father to guide her," she said more softly. "She depends on me to launch her on the sea of matrimony and I have no notion where to begin."

Ogden glowered, started to speak, stopped, started once more. "A young lady today," he said, "needs little help. She shamelessly sets her cap for a gentleman much as those maids were pursuing the flies infesting the drawing room. She chooses her victim, she sets her sights, she takes aim, and *splat,* the young man falls limp and unprotesting, to become imprisoned in the jar of so-called wedded bliss."

Prudence sighed. "Even if what you say were true, Justine lacks the requisite skills. She may be proficient with a bow and arrow but not in the hunting of the male of our species."

Ogden harrumphed his disbelief.

Daphne stood and walked over to Ogden, stopping inches away to look up at him. He edged away, staring at her in some alarm, his astonished gaze fastening

116

on the mystic symbols embroidered on the wide, flowing sleeves of her robelike gown.

"I do love your cravat," she murmured, "but it appears to have become shockingly askew." She slid her hands up across the lapels of his waistcoat to the errant cravat. "May I?" she asked innocently.

Color flooded Ogden's face. He stepped back, his hand going protectively to his throat. "Perfectly capable of adjusting my own cravat," he muttered, swinging around and looking up into the gilt-framed glass. After several minutes of largely ineffectual adjustments to his cravat, he turned to them again.

"I beseech you to help us, Mr. Stewart," Daphne said, her imploring gaze suggesting he represented their one last hope. "We know so little of London and, since London is the world, we know little of the world. While you know so very very much."

Appearing flustered, Ogden sat down heavily in an upholstered chair. He touched the knot in his cravat, then ran his hand through his thick white hair. "In my day," he said, "when a group such as this gathered for a particular purpose, whether in the interest of charity or business or pleasure, they immediately formed themselves into a society or a club."

"A club with but four members?" Gerard protested.

"I do believe," Daphne said, "we should do as Ogden—may I call you Ogden on such a brief acquaintance?—has suggested."

Gerard raised his eyebrows but offered no further objection.

"I agree with Daphne," Prudence said with a shy nod. "But even a small society requires a name. What shall we call ourselves?"

Ogden broke the ensuing silence. "Since our object is to identify and then recruit an acceptable gentleman to seek the hand of Miss Justine Riggs, I propose we call ourselves"—he glanced slyly at each of them in turn—"the Matrimonial Recruitment Society."

After a pause, Daphne laughed delightedly. "How terribly clever, Ogden, since the initials of our society will spell MRS and that is precisely the goal we have in mind for Justine. A wonderful suggestion."

Ogden's gruff harrumphs failed to conceal his pleasure at being praised.

Prudence lowered her voice to a conspiratorial whisper. "We must keep our Matrimonial Recruitment Society a secret. As you must be aware, Justine is a most independent young lady and, at times, is inclined to be somewhat perverse, so she must never know what we have in mind."

"Agreed," Gerard said. "And if we must form a society, I expect we should select someone to preside over our gatherings, a president. Since she brought us together, I believe it only right and proper that Prudence be our leader." After a murmur of approval, he added, "To my way of thinking, no other officers are required."

"Wait," Ogden objected, "we really need to have a secretary. A secretary is a must, someone to record the minutes of our proceedings, to notify members of meetings and to make arrangements for refreshments. Dreary work but absolutely necessary."

"I have in mind the perfect person for such a task," Prudence said. When she looked at the others they all carefully avoided her gaze. "Our secretary should be Rodgers," she said.

118

"Apparently the man can read and write," Gerard observed, "else you would never have suggested him. But can he be trusted not to spread word of our activities from one end of London to the other? We all know how servants love to gossip."

"As you say, he can read and write," Prudence said. "Furthermore, in all his years with me Rodgers has never betrayed a confidence."

Gerard tugged at the tasseled bell pull. "Then, by all means, let us summon Rodgers here."

When Rodgers made his appearance, Gerard handed him a ledger and a quill, explained his duties and seated him in front of the writing desk.

"We wish to accomplish two things," Prudence said hesitantly. "First we must select a gentleman who possesses an unimpeachable character, an appropriate station in life—neither too toplofty nor too common—and having sufficient means to be an acceptable suitor for the hand of Justine Riggs. After we decide on the gentleman, we must arrange for him to meet Justine and thereafter provide as many opportunities as possible to allow acquaintance to blossom into love."

"Agreed," Gerard said. "May I suggest we begin by creating a listing of eligible gentlemen, a pool of marriageable gentlemen if you will, while refraining for the present from debating either their merits or their demerits. When we have gathered five or six names, we will proceed to choose the most likely suitor."

His suggestion was greeted with a murmur of assent.

"I still harbor hope for John Willoughby," Daphne said. "Since Justine has shown herself to be a typical

119

Aries and young Willoughby is a Gemini, they should prove to be wonderfully compatible."

"Willoughby will be placed on our list." Gerard glanced at Rodgers. "Do you have that, Rodgers?"

Rodgers looked up from writing in the ledger. "I do," he assured them, reading his entry: "Mr. John Willoughby."

"I have a second suggestion," Daphne told them. "Only last month I received an unexpected visit from a Mr. Richard Ewing, a young gentleman who anticipates coming into a living in Islington within the next few months. Since he will soon be able to support a family—he spoke of seven children as his ideal—he sought my advice in selecting a bride. Mr. Ewing would be an excellent prospect for Justine."

"I would expect a parson to seek advice through prayer rather than from a reading of the stars." Gerard's tone showed him to be skeptical regarding Mr. Ewing's common sense.

"I find nothing unusual in what Mr. Ewing did," Daphne insisted. "After all, Gerard, as Genesis informs us, God did create the heavens as well as the Earth."

"I believe we agreed, and at your suggestion," Ogden interposed with a speaking glance at Gerard, "to defer debate on the individuals we propose until we have compiled a list of five or six possibilities. So I suggest we put Mr. Ewing's name on the list along with Mr. Willoughby's and go forward."

"Quite right," Gerard said, "I stand corrected. As it happens, I have an unmarried cousin, a Lt. Claude Edgerton, who is presently in London on leave from his regiment. Not only does he show every promise of having an eminently successful military career, he is also distantly connected, on his mother's side, to none other than Lady Jersey."

"Capital!" Ogden nodded. "And I propose we add the name of Mr. Sebastian Cloverly, the bookseller with a shop at 157 Piccadilly."

"Are booksellers and other tradesmen now considered gentlemen?" Gerard, genuinely puzzled, wanted to know. "In my day they were ranked slightly above actors and others of that ilk."

"While I cannot speak for all booksellers," Ogden said, "Mr. Sebastian Cloverly is indeed a gentleman and should be considered." He glanced at Rodgers to make certain he was recording the name. "To recapitulate, we now have four candidates, my nephew, a prospective parson, a military officer and a bookseller. Do any of you have other possibilities?"

They frowned, one and all, lowering their heads in thought. After a lengthy pause, Prudence said, "Another name occurs to me, the son of a friend of my late husband, dear Eustace, although I hesitate to mention his name since I have no notion as to whether he is in England at present or whether he might be at all interested in marriage. He is, however, the sort of gentleman who would, I feel absolutely certain, appreciate Justine's spirit and penchant for independent thinking."

"By all means tell us who he is," Daphne said.

"His name is Mr. Gavin Spencer."

"Gavin Spencer!" Gerard exclaimed. "I should have thought of Spencer myself since years ago I knew his mother, Lavinia, quite well, and Gavin himself has a country house not fifteen miles from here."

"Is he by any chance the same Gavin Spencer who so distinguished himself in the Peninsula Campaign?" Daphne asked. "That Spencer was introduced to me once at the opera and I thought him to be the most handsome and the most dashing man I ever saw. And quite untouched by scandal of any kind."

"Is this the same Spencer who swam the Hellespont a few years ago?" Ogden wanted to know, "to emulate Leander who foolishly braved the dangerous sea, time and again, to be with his love, Hero? And finally drowned as a result of his foolishness?"

"The very same," Gerard said. "The last report of his whereabouts, and this was almost a year ago, placed him in Egypt leading an expedition to seek the source of the Nile. Not only is Gavin Spencer adventurous, handsome and dashing, not only is he a man possessing a rare *savoire faire,* he is also a renowned collector of antiquities, his published accounts of his travels were very well received and, by no means least, he has a considerable fortune inherited only recently from his uncle."

"This Spencer must be a true paragon among men," Ogden said. "If all you claim for him is true."

"To my knowledge, which I admit is limited," Gerard said, "he is a man without faults. He comes closer than anyone in England, with the exception of the Duke of Wellington, to being a legend in his own time."

Ogden shook his head in disbelief. "The man has flaws, rest assured of that, all men do."

"He does have a flaw," Prudence said, "but one that admirably suits our purpose. Gavin Spencer is unmarried, or was at last report."

"If he *is* all you claim," Ogden objected, "which I very much doubt, how strange he has failed to sweep all the young ladies of the *ton* off their feet."

"He is, perhaps," Daphne said, "too occupied with his manly pursuits to have found time for marriage."

"Or he may consider our English young ladies too tame for his taste," Prudence suggested.

"Vincent, his father," Gerard said, "was considered to be as mad as a hatter, being overly fond of both the ladies and whiskey and prepared to risk his all on the turn of a single card. Fortunately for his family, Vincent died well before his time and I suspect his son vowed to be as little like his father as possible."

"Since our interest is in the son and not the father," Ogden grumbled, "you should, I suppose, make inquiries about the man and his whereabouts."

"I shall and at once," Gerard promised. "Though Gavin Spencer appears to be our preeminent prospect he may very well be unavailable. We should, therefore, decide which one of these other gentlemen best suits our purposes."

There followed a chorus of objections.

"But how can I possibly decide?" Daphne asked, "since I am acquainted only with John Willoughby and Mr. Richard Ewing."

"And I," Ogden said, "have no personal knowledge of any of these gentlemen with the exception of my nephew and Mr. Cloverly, the bookseller. And you, Gerard, can only vouch for your lieutenant. What we require is someone, presumably someone younger, more of an age with the candidates, someone with a broad acquaintanceship as well as the ability to pursue inquiries into the histories and proclivities of these gentlemen."

"What you suggest is undoubtedly on the mark," Gerard agreed, "but where are we to find someone in a position to judge their character, their means and their all-around suitability?

There was a general shaking of heads.

Rodgers broke the lengthening silence. "May I," he asked, "presume to offer a suggestion?"

The four members of the Matrimonial Recruitment Society turned to stare at their secretary. Prudence spoke first. "Of course you may, Rodgers," she said. "And what is your suggestion?"

"There is a gentlemen," he told them, "with a wide acquaintanceship in the *ton* who would, I believe, although I cannot guarantee, be more than willing to offer his services to help you focus your attentions on the right man. And, by great good fortune, he happens to be readily available. He is, in fact, presently a guest in this very house."

"You have us all at sea," Prudence said. "Pray tell us his name."

Rodgers smiled. "Why," he said, "he is none other than Lord Devon."

Nine

Quentin guided his horse toward the hedgerow, letting the stallion set his own pace—Quentin was not one to rush his fences—felt the roan's fluid leap, thrilled to the exhilarating ascent, heard hooves scrape the uppermost branches and then they were over, the roan hitting the ground and, in one motion, galloping on to where John Willoughby, astride a dappled grey colt, waited.

"Well done," John said as they swung around and, urging their mounts into a lope, started back to the Manor.

They rode for a time in companionable silence with the noon sun warm on their faces. Entering a lane, they slowed their horses to a walk, listening to the hum of bees as they breathed in the sweet scent of the wild roses growing at the borders of fields divided into irregular rectangles by hedges of shrubs and trees.

"I suppose the eclipse was all very well," John said, "but, to my way of thinking, a rather overrated spectacle, certainly no great thing. Not by any means the sight I expected."

"The rarity of an eclipse is what makes it so extraordinary," Quentin said. "Imagine if the moon rose only once every twenty years, what an eagerly awaited, awe-inspiring sight it would be. How Justine—" He stopped abruptly to correct himself. "How Miss Riggs would savor such an event."

John shook his head and smiled ruefully. "She possesses a formidable knowledge of the heavens. Almost too formidable for my taste. Did she lecture you, Quentin, on the Latin names of the constellations?"

"No, she hardly spoke a word to me all evening."

Because, Quentin thought, *I never gave her the slightest opportunity. How strange that following an impulse can have such disturbing consequences. Kissing her under the stars during the dark of the moon was merely a sudden notion, certainly nothing I planned or premeditated. I meant to do whatever I could to disconcert her, I expect, to put her in her proper place after the audacious way she threatened to use me as a target for her arrows. And all I succeeded in doing was to disconcert myself . . .*

"When I traveled to Gravesend last month," John said, "and saw her walking like a lovely phantom in the night, I admit being somewhat taken with her. But the better acquainted we become, the more uneasy she makes me. I must admit I much prefer a young lady whose company I find restful rather than alarming. A young lady who attempts to please rather than instruct."

"As I do," Quentin said, "as I most certainly do."

When I marry, and I expect I shall in the fullness of time, I intend to choose an amiable beauty with perhaps a touch of the coquette in her nature, a uni-

versal favorite of the ton, *a miss who understands that I, like the overwhelming majority of men, prefer a companion who listens rather than lectures, a young lady who quietly but sincerely applauds my wit and admires the way I sit a horse rather than a hoyden who constantly challenges me.*

"Alton, on the other hand," John said, "appeared quite taken with Justine. Did you notice how he interceded in your behalf at the archery contest? And during the eclipse he was constantly finding excuses to be with her."

"And did she encourage him?" Quentin frowned when he heard the annoyance in his voice.

"She seemed to neither encourage nor discourage him. Justine has a happy way of treating everyone with equal consideration."

"Equal lack of consideration might be closer to the truth." Quentin frowned. "Someone should warn her about Alton, preferably her sponsor. Surely Mrs. Baldwin must be aware of his less than admirable reputation where young women are concerned. His behavior toward Miss Georgiana Moore was abominable; no wonder she saw fit to throw herself into the Serpentine."

John raised his eyebrows. "Surely you exaggerate. Alton is neither better nor worse than most gentlemen of the *ton.*"

"Then may the Lord help the *ton.* And England as well."

A word to Rodgers will serve to alert Prudence Baldwin to the danger. Is it possible Justine has a tenderness for Alton? No, impossible, even a young

127

lady from Gravesend should be capable of discerning that his intentions are less than honorable.

"You surprise me," John said. "I never knew you to be so eager to protect the chastity of a young woman before."

Quentin gave a start. *Why am I so concerned about her well-being?* he asked himself. "Despite her bravado," he said, "Miss Riggs seems innocent and naive."

"In all likelihood Justine will marry before harm befalls her."

Yes, she should marry and undoubtedly will. Why do I find the notion so unappealing? Marriage will not only provide her with a safe haven from the likes of Alton, it will banish her from my thoughts for good and all. From this day forward, I shall do whatever I can do to bring about such a happy solution.

They left the park and approached the house, riding between the kitchen garden and the overgrown maze. As they entered the stable yard Quentin thought he caught a glimpse of someone coming out of the rear door of the Manor.

Leaving their horses with two stableboys, they started toward the great house. Quentin suddenly stopped, for, without knowing why, he was certain, absolutely certain, that it was Justine he had seen leaving the house and that she was now waiting for him at the entrance to the maze.

Walking past one of the barns, he looked toward the maze and drew in his breath. Someone was standing there, watching him, perhaps waiting for him, but when he saw it was Rodgers and not Justine he felt

128

You
can enjoy
more of
the newest
and best
Regency
Romance
novels.
Subscribe
now and…

**GET
3 FREE
REGENCY
ROMANCE
NOVELS–
A $11.97
VALUE!**

TAKE ADVANTAGE OF THIS SPECIAL OFFER, AVAILABLE *ONLY* TO ZEBRA REGENCY ROMANCE READERS.

You are a reader who enjoys the very special kind of love story that can only be found in Zebra Regency Romances. You adore the fashionable English settings, the sparkling wit, the captivating intrigue, and the heart-stirring romance that are the hallmarks of each Zebra Regency Romance novel.

Now, you can have these delightful novels delivered right to your door each month and never have to worry about missing a new book. Zebra has made arrangements through its Home Subscription Service for you to preview the three latest Zebra Regency Romances as soon as they are published.

3 **FREE** REGENCIES TO GET STARTED!

To get your subscription started, we will send your first 3 books ABSOLUTELY FREE, as our introductory gift to you. NO OBLIGATION. We're sure that you will enjoy these books so much that you will want to read more of the very best romantic fiction published today.

SUBSCRIBERS SAVE EACH MONTH

Zebra Regency Home Subscribers will save money each month as they enjoy their latest Regencies. As a subscriber you will receive the 3 newest titles to preview FREE for ten days. Each shipment will be at least a $11.97 value (publisher's price). But home subscribers will be billed only $9.90 for all three books. You'll save over $2.00 each month. Of course, if you're not satisfied with any book, just return it for full credit.

FREE HOME DELIVERY

Zebra Home Subscribers get free home delivery. There are never any postage, shipping or handling charges. No hidden charges. What's more, there is no minimum number to buy and you can cancel your subscription at any time. No obligation and no questions asked.

TO GET YOUR 3 FREE BOOKS
LL OUT AND MAIL THE COUPON BELOW

Mail to: Zebra Regency Home Subscription Service
120 Brighton Road
P.O. Box 5214
Clifton, New Jersey 07015-5214

YES! Start my Regency Romance Home Subscription and send me my 3 FREE BOOKS as my introductory gift. Then each month, I'll receive the 3 newest Zebra Regency Romances to preview FREE for ten days. I understand that if I'm not satisfied, I may return them and owe nothing. Otherwise, I'll pay the low members' price of just $9.90 for all 3 books and save over $2.00 off the publisher's price (a $11.97 value). There are no shipping, handling or other hidden charges. I may cancel my subscription at any time and there is no minimum number to buy. In any case, the 3 FREE books are mine to keep regardless of what I decide.

NAME _____

ADDRESS _____ APT NO. _____

CITY _____ STATE _____ ZIP _____

TELEPHONE (____) _____

SIGNATURE _____

(if under 18 parent or guardian must sign)

RG0993

Terms and prices subject to change. Orders subject to acceptance by Zebra Home Subscription Service, Inc.

GET
3 FREE
REGENCY
ROMANCE
NOVELS—
A $11.97
VALUE!

a pang of dismay and then a shock of surprise at the extent of his disappointment.

With a slight beckoning motion, Rodgers asked Quentin to come to him and so, after walking a short distance with John, Quentin suddenly stopped and, with a muttered curse and the excuse of having forgotten something, turned back while telling John to go on to the house.

"Lord Devon," Rodgers said when Quentin joined him, "I was hoping to intercept you after your ride. If you could grant me a few minutes of your time? Perhaps we might stroll into the maze?"

Quentin nodded and Rodgers led the way into the ancient, overgrown labyrinth of yews. "I trust you can find your way," Quentin said.

"When I arrived here, Mr. Hodgkins, the Kinsdale butler, informed me the maze followed the Hampton Court pattern which, as you no doubt are aware, my lord, permits one to reach the center by going left on entering, right at the next two intersections and then constantly to the left until one reaches his objective."

"Your knowledge continues to amaze me," Quentin said.

"My only goal in life is to put my meager abilities to use in the service of my employers."

Quentin frowned but, unable to see Rodger's face, was unable to estimate the extent of his sincerity. "Someone once remarked," Quentin said, "that judging by the virtues commonly expected of a servant, he knew few masters who would make worthy valets."

"That may be true, my lord, but I have not the slightest doubt you would be an exceptional valet."

"Thank you, Rodgers, for the compliment." He

smiled wryly. "At least I believe it was a compliment."

Before Rodgers could reply, they came to the center of the maze, a circular opening among the yews. Walking past a sundial, Quentin turned and put a booted foot on one of the two iron benches.

"May I speak to you in confidence?" Rodgers, who had remained standing, asked. When Quentin nodded, Rodgers went on, "You will be approached shortly, in all likelihood later today, by Mr. Kinsdale who will request your help in a rather delicate matter."

Quentin raised his eyebrows but said nothing.

"It seems that Mr. Kinsdale and some of his friends have given themselves the task of finding a suitable marriage partner for Miss Riggs."

Quentin stared. How strange, only minutes before he had been thinking along much the same lines. "And why would they approach me? Surely they would never consider me to be a—"

"No, no, not at all. You must forgive me, my lord, I failed to make myself clear. They have compiled a list of possible suitors and want you to give them the benefit of your considered opinion on the merits and demerits of each of the gentlemen." Rodgers drew a paper from his pocket and unfolded it. "I have here a list of the five gentlemen in question together with a few of my own comments regarding their characters and prospects."

"Pray let me scan your list." Taking the paper from Rodgers, Quentin glanced at the names. "Willoughby, I know him, of course; Cloverly, the bookseller, I know who he is since I happen to patronize his shop; Edgerton, a passing acquaintance of mine, recently bought a commission, I believe; Ewing, I fear the name means nothing to me; Spencer—Gavin Spencer, the explorer and adventurer?—in Egypt the last I heard." He looked up from the list. "These notes of yours following the names, these comments that will allow me to steal a march on Mr. Kinsdale, how did you come by these judgments, Rodgers?"

"My informants must remain confidential, my lord, but you must realize that most of the talk below stairs concerns the doings of those above stairs. And, with the large number of my fellow servants gathered here for the eclipse party, my sources are numerous."

"Am I right in assuming," Quentin said, folding the paper and putting it into his pocket, "that you have a favorite among these prospects, a gentleman you yourself would recommend to Miss Riggs?"

"I admit to a slight leaning, an inclination, a tendency in a particular direction." Rodgers, as though resisting temptation, shook his head. "However, I must not interfere, my place is to humbly serve others, not to advise them."

Quentin smiled. "You lead me to the center of this maze, you present me with a list of gentlemen together with brief descriptions of their strengths and failings, and then you tell me you refuse to advise or to recommend. You, Rodgers, are nothing but a humbug."

Rodgers lowered his head. "If you say so, sir, it must be so." Looking up, he asked, "You will help Mr. Kinsdale and,the others find an appropriate suitor for Miss Riggs?"

Quentin paused in thought. "I see no harm in doing so." In all truth, the notion rather appealed to him.

"Very good, I hoped you would, and I wish you

success." Rodgers stepped back to let Quentin lead the way from the maze. As they walked along the intricately winding pathway, Rodgers said, seemingly apropos of nothing, "Miss Riggs told me yesterday about a red-haired stableboy she befriended."

"Oh?" Quentin was unsure what Rodgers meant to tell him.

"The boy was having trouble with a fractious horse that kicked in the side of his stall. Miss Riggs asked me to help if I could, and, in the course of our conversation, I learned that since coming here to the Manor, she has been in the habit of riding to Round Hill at half past eight every morning."

When Quentin glanced back at him with a questioning frown, Rodgers said, "My remarks about the red-haired stableboy and Miss Riggs were of no consequence, my lord, I was merely attempting to fill a void in the conversation."

"Were you indeed?" Quentin murmured. "I wonder."

"As well as, of course," Rodgers added somewhat hastily, "hinting at the possibility that Mr. Willoughby might care to be apprised of an opportunity to become better acquainted with the young lady."

A perfectly reasonable suggestion, Quentin told himself, though where John was concerned, probably completely useless. He eyed Rodgers assessingly as they left the maze and made their way to the house. The man's thinking took more twists and turns than the corridors in the maze. Was it possible Rodgers had something more devious in mind?

"Have you, by any chance," he asked, "mentioned

Miss Riggs's morning rides to anyone else? To Lord Alton, for instance?"

"Why no, my lord, certainly not. As you are aware, Lord Alton's name does not appear on Mr. Kinsdale's list of possible suitors."

"Quite so," Quentin said, wondering what had led him to mention Alton, since Justine could never hope to reach so high. Even if she were more favorably situated, Alton was not an appropriate choice, not at all.

Later that afternoon, Gerard Kinsdale approached Quentin. "If you could grant me but a few minutes," he said, "I seek your counsel on a matter of the greatest delicacy."

When Quentin readily agreed, Gerard led his guest into the library, carefully closing the door behind them. As Quentin waited with mounting exasperation, Gerard paced nervously in front of the hearth, rambling on about the eclipse and then recalling a long-ago shooting party at Meachams where he'd had the good fortune to meet both Quentin's father and uncle.

Quentin nodded. "The matter of the greatest delicacy?" he prodded.

"I—that is, we—would greatly appreciate, and I shall put the matter bluntly, your help in selecting an appropriate suitor for Miss Justine Riggs."

Raising his eyebrows to feign surprise, Quentin let a moment pass before he said, "I shall do my best to help you."

"Capital!" Gerard sat opposite Quentin and leaned toward him. "We would value your opinion of our five prospects," he told the younger man. "Any information you pass on, I give you my solemn oath, will go no further. My lips will be forever sealed."

Quentin nodded. He would, he had decided after his tête-à-tête with Rodgers in the maze, be as forthcoming and impartial with his advice as he possibly could. His goal, after all, was the same as Gerard's—to see Justine speedily and happily wed.

"The first gentleman we wish to consider," Gerard said, "is your friend, Mr. John Willoughby."

"An excellent young man, a boon companion with an amiable disposition, a friend to all, a Trojan, a man with excellent prospects, a man of marriageable age who comes from a fine family." Quentin sighed. "Regrettably, I must inform you of a conversation John and I had earlier today in which he stated emphatically that he had absolutely no romantic interest in Miss Riggs. I fear you must cross his name from your list."

"I suspected as much." Taking a paper from his pocket and resting it on the arm of his chair, Gerard drew a firm line through the name of John Willoughby. "The next name," he went on, "is that of Mr. Richard Ewing, a young gentleman who is assured of coming into a living in Islington within the next month or two."

"Under normal circumstances, a young parson would be a capital choice for Miss Riggs. However, to call your Mr. Ewing young is to use that word in the loosest possible sense since he will never see forty again. Mr. Ewing turned to the solace of religion somewhat late in life, it seems, in an attempt to atone for his stupendously dissolute youth. Now he intends to sire a quiverful of children, seven, I believe, a number that may or may not equal the number of byblows he has left scattered across England from Kent to Cornwall. And, or so I understand, he happens to be a garrulous fellow who has been known to drive his dinner companions to tears of boredom while he spoke twaddle without allowing an interruption for over thirty minutes at a time."

Should Justine marry such a man as Richard Ewing? Quentin asked himself. Not if he could prevent it. Never!

Gerard shook his head. "Mr. Ewing will not do," he said with a sigh, striking his name, "and so, with regret, I throw him overboard."

"Your next candidate?" Quentin asked.

"Lt. Claude Edgerton, a cousin of mine."

"Edgerton is a personable gentleman who thoroughly savors life," Quentin said, "although perhaps too much so. Even though he is your cousin, I trust you will take no offense if I speak frankly."

"No, no offense, he's a third cousin, actually. Barely acquainted with the chap."

Nodding, Quentin went on. "Edgerton is, I understand—I cannot speak from personal knowledge—a four-bottle man and a gamester who has become the target of the cent-per-centers. He has the reputation of being a man who makes a habit of voweling debts."

"Voweling debts? Is that cant?"

"It means giving his IOU's to all and sundry. If he fails to drink himself to death, leaving an impoverished widow behind, I expect he may end his days an exile in Calais or some other haven for debtors."

He would never condemn Justine to a marriage with such an utter scoundrel as Claude Edgerton, Quentin told himself. Never!

Without saying a word, Gerard crossed the name of Lieutenant Edgerton from his rapidly shrinking list. "Next," he said, "we have a gentleman who, though some might label him a tradesman, is a man with literary credentials—Mr. Sebastian Cloverly, the bookseller."

"The Cloverly with the shop on Piccadilly? Ah, yes, Cloverly, I know him well, a rather starched though enterprising man of business whose principal income derives from first commissioning the memoirs of aging and impoverished demimondes and then requesting payments from the gentlemen who, in their youth, were overly amorous while at the same time indiscreet, but who are now aging, respectable aristocrats who have no desire to receive unfavorable public attention and so are more than willing to pay large sums to your Mr. Cloverly to have the accounts of their unseemly adventures stricken from his soon-to-be-published manuscripts."

"Oh dear," Gerard murmured, "oh dear, oh dear."

"If this enterprising method of doing business meets with your approval, Mr. Cloverly might prove an excellent prospect for Miss Riggs. Oh, yes, looking at the other side of the coin, the darker side, he does have one somewhat unfortunate characteristic; alas, your Mr. Cloverly is reputed by those close to him to eschew regular bathing and although, to his everlasting credit, he makes frequent and liberal use of a variety of perfumeries, he habitually gives off what was described to me as 'a most unpleasant stench.' "

Quentin wrinkled his nose. Mr. Cloverly would never do for Justine. Never!

"He will never do," Gerard said, echoing Quentin's

thoughts. "Alas and alack, I have only one more name to suggest," he said, "and that is Mr. Gavin Spencer of Prospect Hall, a neighbor of mine."

"I know him only by his reputation which is quite out-of-the-ordinary. Exemplary, in fact. Gavin Spencer is an adventurer and an author, an explorer whose latest expedition set out last year to travel up the Nile seeking the headwaters of that mighty river somewhere in the legendary Mountains of the Moon. From what I hear, he courts danger, almost recklessly risking an untimely end by scaling Alpine peaks during the avalanche season or by swimming the treacherous Hellespont or by risking his life fighting for Wellington on the Peninsula. My one and only reservation is that Mr. Spencer seems almost too much of a good thing. He behaves as though he had something to prove to the rest of us." Quentin shook his head. "If only he were in England! Gavin Spencer is, however, still somewhere in the jungles of central Africa."

Although he could not be certain why, Quentin was quite unable to picture Justine married to Gavin Spencer despite Spencer's sterling character. Fortunately, Spencer was many miles from English shores.

Gerard stared down at his list as he sadly shook his head. "We must," he said as, rising, he returned the list to his pocket, "give this matter additional thought. Perhaps you, Quentin, could suggest a suitable gentleman for us to consider."

Quentin closed his eyes and pursed his lips as he made every effort to think of a likely prospect. No, try as he might, there was no one he could imagine being married to Justine Riggs. "As of now, no," he said, "but if a name occurs to me I shall most certainly inform you at once."

The two men left the library and were descending the great staircase when Quentin saw Ogden Stewart hurrying along the lower hall toward them holding a newspaper aloft. Ogden stopped at the bottom of the stairs and waved the paper exultantly. "Good news!" he called up to them. *"The Times* reports he returned to London last week."

"Who returned to London?" Gerard asked.

Quentin, with a feeling of dismay he found difficult to explain, seemed to know the answer to Gerard's question even before Ogden said, "Why, Mr. Gavin Spencer, of course. And he intends to come to Prospect Hall for an extended stay."

Ten

There was, Justine sensed, something in the air at Kinsdale Manor, something concerning herself or so the overheard murmur of voices told her, the buzz of whispered conversations behind unfurled fans followed by sudden silences when she made her appearance. She found herself the object of covert glances, of knowing nods and speculative and appraising stares.

Is something truly amiss, she asked herself, or am I only imagining there is? She had, admittedly, been restless of late and subject to idle fancies. Ever since the night of the eclipse she had been all at sea, far out of her depth, as though she had waded into the calm ocean from the beach at Brighton and, all at once stepped into a bottomless trough where she discovered herself flailing her arms and legs to keep afloat.

The fault lay entirely with Quentin Fletcher. No, not Quentin, why did she continue to think of him in such a familiar fashion? To her he was now and would be henceforth Lord Devon. But whether she thought of him formally or not, thinking of him agitated her senses, bringing new and altogether strange longings to life. Clenching her hands, she drew in a series of deep breaths as she willed herself not to dwell on what had happened on Round Hill.

There was no doubt that Lord Devon had behaved abominably; her every feeling had been offended. He had acted as he had, to avenge himself for her having had the temerity to challenge him in the race in the park. Why else would he have taken such liberties? Evidently he believed himself to be a second Lord Byron whose very presence caused women to swoon in helpless adoration. What foolishness! If this was what Lord Devon believed, he was very much mistaken, at least as far as she was concerned.

She must, though, be completely honest with herself. She had, shamelessly—if only for the briefest of instants—returned his kiss. But only because he had taken her by surprise, stalking her while concealed by the darkness of the eclipse.

Justine drew in her breath. True, the night had been very dark but was it possible that someone had, unbeknownst to her, seen him gather her into his arms, seen Quentin kiss her? Was that the reason Prudence and Daphne, and Ogden and Gerard as well, seemed to share a secret, a secret that concerned her?

Just this morning, shortly after breakfast, Justine had glimpsed Ogden showing Daphne an item in *The Times*. On seeing Justine, he hastily folded the newspaper and put it aside. Later she had retrieved the paper but when she scanned its contents—a naval skirmish with the United States, a speech by Henry "Orator" Hunt, the unbounded public enthusiasm for the visiting German General Blücher and the return

140

to England from North Africa of the explorer Gavin Spencer—she found nothing that could possibly concern her.

How puzzling.

Never one to fret silently, that evening Justine sought out Prudence, found her in the drawing room and came directly to the point. "I suspect," she said, "that you and Daphne and others as well are talking about me behind my back."

The older woman's hands flew to cover her mouth; she looked at the ceiling, at the floor, to the right and to the left but never at Justine. She stammered as she said, "You believe that Daphne and I . . . that Ogden and Gerard and I that all four of us . . . are somehow involved in some connivance having to do with you? Whatever in the world gave you such a notion?"

Justine told her all she had observed.

"*The Times?* Whispered conversations behind fans?" Prudence sat down heavily on a couch and, despite the coolness of the evening, proceeded to vigorously fan herself. "My heart is all aflutter," she said. "I feel quite faint."

Justine waited patiently until, as she knew would happen, Prudence regained some measure of composure.

"When you came to me from Gravesend," the older woman said at last, "I pledged to myself to see you properly married. As, on more than one occasion, I believe I told you."

"True enough," Justine said.

"However, and despite the best efforts of your tutor, M. Lambert, and myself, all my plans seemed to come to nought and so, I must admit, I did request the help

141

of certain of my friends and they kindly consented, for my sake and for yours, to come to my aid."

Justine stared at her, aghast and angry. "All four of you—? Seeking ways to marry me off—? Am I so lacking in the feminine graces that I require the urgent attentions of two gentlemen and two ladies in addition to a tutor?"

Prudence sighed. "Our only intent was, and is, to take the place of the mother you unfortunately never had. You *are* of a marriageable age, Justine, and you must admit you have few if any prospects."

Shamed despite herself but at the same time vexed, Justine bit back an angry answer, turned and half-ran and half-walked from the drawing room. Starting up the stairs, she abruptly changed her mind and, seeking the open air, hurried through the Blue Room to the terrace where she stood with her hands gripping the back of a bench that faced the downward slope of the side lawn.

As her anger slowly ebbed, tears of frustration and self-pity stung her eyes. Everything Prudence had said about her was right, she was a complete and absolute failure. As a woman. She could not blame her father for her failure, since he had loved her and raised her as best he knew how. No, it was totally her fault. She could and did observe how other young ladies her age behaved and yet she did not try to emulate them.

As she well knew, a young lady's foremost duty in life was to seek and find a suitable gentleman who would woo and win her hand and, hopefully, her heart. She had not found such a man, seemingly she would never find one and, therefore, she was hopeless.

Justine looked overhead and saw, through a rift in

the scudding clouds, a single star twinkling in the northern sky, probably the North Star, reminding her of the many times she had, in years past, gazed at the North Star as she imagined wayfarers all around the globe viewing it that very same moment and depending on its unvarying position above the pole to guide them as they sailed across uncharted seas or trekked through unmapped lands.

She had always longed to travel, to America, perhaps, or to the exotic Orient or to Australia to view the southern constellations. But she had never in her eighteen years journeyed more than sixty miles from where she stood at this very moment. She had often watched ships set sail from Gravesend bound for foreign ports, for Constantinople, for Singapore, for Rio de Janeiro, for Philadelphia and for Cape Town, and she had dreamed of being on board those ships, of crossing the sea to places she had never been where she would witness sights she had only imagined.

Someday I will journey to other lands, she had promised herself, and she repeated that pledge now. The heavens, wondrous as they were, could only be viewed from afar but this immense and infinitely varied world, this Earth, could be explored by anyone intrepid enough to challenge the unknown, by anyone willing to forsake the comforts of hearth and home. She might never be able to attract a suitable husband but she did have the courage and the will to travel. How foolish she had been to pity herself.

As she watched, clouds swept across the North Star, leaving the heavens dark. A dog barked in the Manor kennel, from the stables came the neigh of a horse and then the summer night was silent. With a sigh of regret for her deferred dream of journeying into the unknown but with a renewed determination to make that dream come true sooner rather than later, Justine returned to the house.

She must, Justine told herself, go to Prudence forthwith and apologize for her unseemly behavior. Prudence *did* mean well.

The curling thread of a ballad played on a pianoforte drew her from the Blue Room into the great hall and then along the hall toward the brightly lighted music room. The door was open and, as she approached and heard an underlying murmur of voices and soft laughter, she recalled that a musical evening had been planned.

Pausing just outside the doorway, her eyes were drawn not to the attractive fair-haired young lady playing the piano—her name, Justine recalled, was Phillippa—nor to the vase of pink and white daisies on the piano behind the music rack nor to the niche in the wall behind Phillippa with its statue of a partially garbed Diana walking with a dog at her side, the huntress' flowing robes draped to expose her breasts and bare her left leg to the thigh, but rather to Quentin Fletcher who sat on the piano bench beside Phillippa, his gaze intent on her lovely face as he absently turned the sheets of music for her.

Phillippa, her pink lips slightly parted, her eyes almost closed, her golden hair circled by a pearl coronet matching the single strand of pearls encircling her neck, wore a flowing white silk gown that bared her shoulders and the upper curves of her breasts.

Justine's throat tightened and she felt the sting of tears. Determined not to cry, even though she felt herself to be a stranger alone in a strange land, she turned her back on the soft glow of the lamps, the lilt of laughter and the gentle strains of the ballad that spoke to her of a hopeless, unrequited love.

Walking dispiritedly away from the music room she came face to face with Daphne Gauthier. Not wanting to talk to anyone, Justine nodded and stepped to one side, only to have Daphne place a hand on her wrist.

"Come with me," Daphne said after glancing beyond Justine at the open door to the music room. "I must tell you about my dream since it concerns you, Justine, and your future."

Without waiting for a yes or no, Daphne turned and led Justine to her room in the east wing of the Manor where she sat at her dressing table, her back to the mirror, and waved Justine to a high-backed white and gold chair.

"When I napped this afternoon," Daphne said, "I had the most unusual dream. I saw a long ship, a ship with a single square sail the color of the sun, and a prow fashioned in the shape of a red dragon's head. More than a score of warriors manned the ship's oars, thrusting the vessel through the waves. A chieftain stood in the prow, a tall stalwart warrior with hair the color of wheat." The light from the candle on the table by the bed glistened in Daphne's eyes as she recalled her dream. "The warrior's magnificent bronzed chest was bared to the wind and to the spray from the sea, the sun glinted from his horned helmet and from the unsheathed sword he held aloft in his right hand. In his other hand he carried a round, painted shield."

"You seem to be describing a Viking," Justine said,

her interest caught despite her skepticism. "Is that what he was?"

"He may well have been," she said, waving the question away as unimportant. "The warriors, Vikings or whatever they were, beached their ship on a pebbled strand and their chieftain led them ashore, ransacking a village, an English village, and setting it ablaze with the fire from their torches. The chieftain left his men to their plunderings, climbing a promontory overlooking the sea and there, at the crest, came to a strange structure, a small gazebolike building with a walkway around all four sides."

Daphne was describing, Justine realized with a start of recognition, her observatory in Gravesend.

"I knew, as you sometimes know in dreams, that you, Justine, had taken refuge inside the gazebo, bolting the single door. Mere locks and bolts could never stop this man. He stepped back, raised his foot and kicked the door open. You screamed. You fought him. You clawed at his face. All to no avail. He swept you into his arms and carried you through the burning village to his ship and sailed into the mist."

Justine gazed at her, fascinated. "And then?"

Daphne shook her head. "That was the end of my dream. As the ship drew away from shore, I awoke and sat up in bed, my heart pounding."

"A Viking warrior raiding the English coast and carrying me off to sea," Justine mused. "A very strange dream. What could it possibly mean?"

"Perhaps nothing at all. Or, and I suspect this is the case, it could be a portent. Is a stranger coming into your life from across the sea? A Scandinavian?

146

A warrior chieftain suggests the military. Will he be an officer? All we can do is wait and see."

A Scandinavian? An officer? Recalling Daphne's earlier prediction that John Willoughby was the gentleman destined to win her hand, Justine barely refrained from voicing her doubts about this supposed portent. Such foolishness! Why had she allowed herself to be drawn into Daphne's theatric though undoubtedly false vision? No warrior was about to appear from across the sea to make her his captive and carry her off in his arms.

"I understand how skeptical you must be," Daphne said quietly, leaning forward and covering Justine's hand with her own. "You happen to be a most fetching young lady," she said, "and yet you seem to hold yourself in low esteem. At least where men are concerned."

"Men may have never given me reason not to."

"Have you ever stopped to consider," Daphne asked, "how strange it is that so many gentlemen have rather outsized ears?"

Puzzled by this unexpected turn of their conversation, Justine could only stare at Daphne. A disproportionate number of men with large ears? Pausing to recollect the proportions of the ears of the men of her acquaintance, she was forced to admit that John Willoughby, Ogden Stewart and Lord Alton all had larger than normal ears.

"There are those that do," Justine said with a question in her voice.

"Just so. And surely they number more than half. In the grand scheme resulting in the creation of the heavens and the Earth, you would expect men to have been given ears of a generous size by their Creator for one purpose and one purpose only. The better to hear, the better to listen. How strange it is that so few of them do. In my experience, they much prefer to talk than to listen, especially in discourse with women."

"Prudence once told me I should never attempt to lecture a man. Or even appear to lecture him."

"She was quite right, you should always give the impression of awaiting a man's every word as though you believed he possessed the wisdom of Solomon spiced by the wit of Sydney Smith and expressed with all of the lyrical gifts of Lord Byron. In other words, as though he were a true paragon."

Justine smiled. "Since such a combination of talents in one person is well nigh impossible, surely any man would recognize the falsity of such flattery."

"Ah, my dear Justine, you give men much too much credit. If you were to follow my advice, instead of suspecting you of deceit a man would credit you with wisdom of the highest order. The only evidence of intelligence a man values in a woman is the intelligence to recognize his merits and to applaud them."

"Do you hold men is such low regard?" Justine asked in surprise.

"Certainly not, I enjoy men, I like being with them and they, or some of them at least, have always seemed to take pleasure in being with me. But to enjoy the company of men does not require one to ignore their faults."

"Surely some gentlemen must appreciate honesty and forthrightness in a woman."

"There may be one somewhere, but in my forty-one

years I have yet to meet him. That, my dear Justine, is the way of this world of ours and, whether we happen to approve or disapprove, we must make the best of it."

Daphne admitted to only forty-one years? Justine smiled to herself, aware this was a white lie. Daphne was definitely a woman of a certain age and that age must be at least fifty. Will I, she wondered, do the same as I grow older? Somehow she thought not.

"Gentlemen do appreciate a young lady with talents," Daphne said. "As long as her talents are feminine ones such as embroidery or the painting of watercolors."

"Or playing the piano."

Daphne gave her an inquiring glance. "Or playing the piano," she repeated. "I understand from Prudence that you, Justine, do possess a talent, that you have a most pleasant singing voice."

"My father always claimed I did. And I enjoy singing."

"Just so. We shall go then, you and I, to the music room where we shall join the others. If you are given the opportunity to sing tonight, you must take it. A young lady must seize every opportunity to show herself off to her best advantage."

"Not tonight, Daphne." Justine put her hand to her forehead. "I feel a fit of the dismals coming on and I really should—"

Daphne held up her hand. "Wait, say no more. There are times for a woman to have megrims and there are times for her not to have megrims. This, it happens, is a time not to have them. You have no reason to be afraid. Are you afraid?"

Justine blinked and raised her chin. "Of course not. Afraid? Not in the least."

"Then we shall make our way to the music room." Daphne rose and started toward the door only to hesitate and return to her dressing table. Picking up a vial, she removed the glass stopper and raised the vial to her nose. "Pure heaven," she murmured, handing the vial to Justine who, after a nod from Daphne, used the stopper to dab the sweet scent on her inner wrists.

"The scent is French violet," Daphne told her, "from Yardleys. English gentlemen, I have found, are especially partial to French violet." When Justine started to return the vial to the dressing table, Daphne said, "You must put scent behind your ears as well."

After Justine did as she was told, Daphne stood back and looked appraisingly at her from head to toe, from the small bow of the blue ribbon holding her curling black hair to her pale blue muslin gown—edged with white ruffles on its V neckline and on its sleeves and hem—to her darker blue slippers. Daphne frowned but then gave a nod as if to say, "Near enough, the clothes will have to do."

Entering the music room during a lull in the entertainment, Daphne immediately led her across the room to Gerard. As Daphne and Gerard exchanged the usual courtesies, Justine glanced around her, noting with satisfaction that Quentin was engaged in earnest conversation with a gentleman she failed to recognize while Phillippa sat on the opposite side of the room amidst a circle of admirers.

Suddenly, to Justine's dismay, she heard Daphne say, "Dear Gerard, Justine would so like to sing for us."

"A capital notion," Gerard said, "and I shall accompany her on the pianoforte." Before she could demur, he led Justine to a helter-skelter stack of music resting atop a sideboard, many of the sheets creased and stained with age. "I have none of the more modern ballads, I fear," he admitted, "but to my mind the old songs have always been the best songs."

Justine leafed through the sheets of music, pausing when she unearthed a collection of sea chanteys. She smiled, recollecting with nostalgic fondness how much her father had loved songs of the forecastle. And, yes, here was one of his favorites.

"You wish to sing 'High Barbaree'?" Gerard asked, reading the title.

When Justine nodded, he hesitated, then placed the music on the rack, sat at the piano and struck a few attention-attracting chords. Quentin, she saw, stood at the hearth, his hand on the fireplace mantel, his gaze on her. She looked quickly away.

As soon as the room quieted, Gerard said, "Miss Riggs will now favor us with a song," and began playing.

At first she sang the familiar melody softly, tentatively:

There were two lofty ships from old England came,

Blow high! Blow low! And so sailed we;

One was the *Prince Rupert* and the other *Prince of Wales* . . .

By the time she came to the chorus her voice had grown clearer and more confident:

Cruising down along the coast of the High Barbaree.

151

She had scarcely begun the second verse when she realized something was amiss. A woman tittered, causing her to look up. Had it been Phillippa? Quentin, his hand covering his mouth, stared at her, his expression unreadable. Was he smiling? Daphne was shaking her head as though saying, "Quite inappropriate."

There was nothing improper about this song telling of Jack tars doing battle with the Barbary Coast pirates, Justine assured herself even as she fought to overcome her baffled chagrin, nothing improper at all. Even so, she skipped several verses to sing the final stanza:

'Oh, quarter! Oh, quarter!' these pirates did cry,
Blow high! Blow low! And so sailed we;
But the quarters that we gave them—we sunk them in the sea,
Cruising down along the coast of the High Barbaree.

As she stopped singing, she heard a collective intake of breath and thought it had to do with her but when she looked around the room she found all eyes directed toward the door. A man had entered, a tall, broad-shouldered, flaxen-haired man, his rugged face tanned by the wind and sun. The women stared at him, fascinated, while the men looked at him with grudging admiration.

There came a murmur as his name was whispered, "Gavin Spencer," and then repeated, "Gavin, Gavin Spencer."

"Bravo," Gavin Spencer cried, his gaze on her. "Bravo!" Striding across the room to a startled Justine, he took her hand and raised it to his lips. "You were magnificent," he told her.

Eleven

They met the next morning, the four conspirators and their trusted aide, the four members of the Matrimonial Recruitment Society and Rodgers, their secretary and majordomo, gathered in the circular, cupola-roofed gazebo situated behind a screen of shrubbery at the bottom of the sloping side lawn of the Manor. Their mood was one of quiet, self-satisfied jubilation.

"Mr. Gavin Spencer," Prudence exulted, "was all I hoped he might be; he even exceeded my fondest expectations. From the moment he entered the music room until he bade us all good night he was the cynosure of all eyes."

"He proved to be more handsome and more impeccably garbed than I remembered him," said Daphne.

"And not in the least vain about his appearance," said Gerard, "although he has every reason to be."

"A gentleman of aristocratic bearing from head to toe," said Prudence.

"And," put in Daphne, "without the least evidence

of pomposity or braggadocio. As ready to listen as he is to speak."

"I admit," said Ogden, "that Mr. Spencer has done more in his thirty-odd years than most men accomplish in a lifetime. The man has uncommon bottom."

"And yet," said Daphne, "he never puts his knowledge, however fascinating, on parade, never marches his vast achievements back and forth before our eyes in order to garner our applause."

"When you spoke to Lord Devon," Prudence said to Gerard, "did he offer any objection whatsoever to Mr. Spencer?"

Ogden looked up as though roused from sleep. "Lord Devon," he said. "A marquess. Do maidens ever visit Birmingham?"

"I beg your pardon?" said Gerard.

"A bit of nonsense I learned as a child to help me remember the five degrees of the nobility in descending order. Duke, marquess, earl, viscount, baron. Do maidens ever visit Birmingham?"

Gerard glowered at him, then shook his head and turned to Prudence. "As to Lord Devon objecting to Mr. Spencer," he said, "he did not. His only remark that might possibly be construed as less than enthusiastic came when he said he thought Mr. Gavin Spencer appeared to be too much of a good thing."

"Admittedly," said Prudence, "all gentlemen have their faults but I believe those of Mr. Spencer must be feather-light when compared to his weighty virtues. And," she added with the rising lilt of enthusiasm, "he appeared quite taken with Justine."

"I watched them," said Ogden. He paused as

154

though to collect his thoughts. "He practically doted on the girl."

"And she," Prudence said hopefully, "seemed to be quite taken with him. Do you agree?"

Daphne raised her eyes to heaven. "At least she had the good sense not to challenge Gavin Spencer to a sporting contest of some sort. I did give her a few words of womanly advice earlier in the evening regarding the proper attitude for a young lady to adopt when in the company of a male of our species. If she takes my words to heart they will, I expect, do her a world of good."

"Does Mr. Spencer leave the Manor to return to Prospect Hall today?" asked Ogden.

Gerard nodded. "He may already have departed," he told them. "Mr. Spencer expects to be in residence at the Hall for several months but he confided to me that he intends to spend much of that time in seclusion while writing an account of his adventures in Africa searching for the headwaters of the Nile."

"It behooves us, then," said Prudence, "to act swiftly and decisively, the better to enhance Justine's prospects."

Daphne smiled rather smugly. "I have already accomplished more along that line than any of you might imagine. Last evening, before Justine and I came to the music room, I told her of my dream."

"Your dream?" the others asked almost in unison.

"In my dream I saw Gavin Spencer as a Viking warlord sailing from the mists of the eastern sea to lead his plundering hordes on a raid along the English coast. Finding Justine alone and unprotected, he swept her into his arms and carried her off in his long boat."

"Mr. Spencer's ancestry does happen to be Danish," said Gerard.

Ogden frowned, started to speak, stopped, began again. "You actually dreamed this, Daphne?" he asked with a thread of skepticism running through his voice.

"Heavens yes, dear Ogden, though this did happen to be a waking dream, a vision if you will. I have them now and again and, more often than not, they serve to lift the veil that conceals the future from our all-too-fallible human eyes."

"And Justine?" Gerard wanted to know. "What did she have to say to this dream of yours?"

"Though she said little or nothing, I could perceive how fascinated she was, how intrigued by my handsome Viking adventurer. I do believe I succeeded in sewing seeds on fertile soil. Last evening the fledgling plant began to send forth tendrils of growth and now only requires our devoted nourishment to finally blossom into the full flower of love."

Ogden rumbled, opened his mouth to speak, paused, then said gruffly, "I was led to believe our object was matrimony, not love."

Daphne leaned toward him and briefly rested the tips of her fingers on his knee. "Dear Ogden," said she, "to me, love is the most important thing in the world; matrimony, on the other hand, is a mere formality, a token nod to the parsons and the solicitors. Given time, I fully intend to make a true believer of you."

"While acknowledging the importance of both love and matrimony," Prudence said, "we must direct our attention to Justine and Mr. Gavin Spencer. Do you, Rodgers, have any suggestions?"

"The poet claims that 'Music has charms to soothe a savage breast,' " Rodgers quoted with a deferential smile, " 'To soften rocks or bend a knotted oak.' If the musical evening truly kindled the first spark of love, perhaps combining the intimacy of dancing with the charms of music will encourage the spark to flame into a veritable conflagration."

"Just so," said Gerard. "As it happens, I have reason to believe something of the sort may very well occur since last night, during my brief conversation with Mr. Spencer, I made two important, nay, to us, two momentous discoveries. The first was that Mr. Spencer has journeyed home to England and to Prospect Hall with one preeminent purpose in mind, namely to search for a suitable wife. I have every reason to believe he will act swiftly and decisively in this matter as he always has in other matters."

"Ahh," Prudence and Daphne murmured.

"And, secondly," Gerard went on, "I learned that Mr. Spencer and his mother will host a costume ball at Prospect Hall on Saturday week. And they intend to invite all of our house party to attend."

"How delightful," said Prudence. She closed her eyes. "Justine Riggs Spencer," she said tentatively. "Justine Spencer," she said with emphasis. "Yes, I do like the sound of it."

Quentin Fletcher mounted Lancelot, a black stallion, and left the stable yard well before eight for an early morning ride across the countryside. When he neared Round Hill, he circled to approach the summit from the south. Nearing the summit, he dismounted and tethered Lancelot, removed a spyglass from his saddlebag and walked to the top of the treeless dome of rock on the crest of the hill.

As he started to raise the spyglass, he paused, recalling the night of the eclipse, reliving once more the moment when he took Justine in his arms and kissed her, remembering, with a self-satisfied smile, the sudden and unexpected fervor with which she had returned that kiss. Quentin shook his head in an attempt to banish his reverie. A single stolen kiss. How trivial an event, how completely insignificant. Why then, he wondered, did he find it impossible to erase that kiss from his thoughts? Why then had he ridden here to Round Hill at the ungodly hour of eight in the morning?

Pushing aside questions for which he had no logical answers, he again raised the spyglass to scan the countryside below him, searching in vain for a lone rider as he shifted the glass from the Manor across the fields cut into tidy rectangles by their hedgerows to another country house some two miles from his vantage point. Prospect Hall. The residence of Mr. Gavin Spencer, damn him. The devil take Gavin Spencer— the man should have stayed in Africa.

Placing his spyglass in a cleft on the rock, Quentin walked the circumference of the Round Hill summit, stopping now and again to look below him. Each time he shook his head in disappointment. Where was she? Rodgers had said she rode this way every morning and Rodgers was seldom wrong. But today there was. no sign of her.

Why am I here? Quentin asked himself. He had no reasonable answer. He had been *compelled* to come to Round Hill by the fever raging in his blood. Like any normal fever, he assured himself, this one would burn itself out in time but for now there was nothing on Earth he could do about it—not that he was at all certain he wanted to.

Time passed and still she did not appear. Annoyed and impatient, he paced back and forth across the summit rock, then returned to his horse fully intending to mount Lancelot and ride back to the Manor. Instead he returned to the crest of the hill and again scanned the country lanes far below. He should, he told himself, abandon this folly. He could not. He must see her. Now.

A bay horse appeared from behind a screen of trees. Quentin caught his breath, and his heart leapt when he recognized Justine garbed in a green habit and riding sidesaddle. And then he groaned and muttered a curse as a second rider came into view immediately behind her. Even from this distance—he estimated it was almost a mile—he could tell it was Gavin Spencer sitting tall and erect astride a white horse looking as proud as a prince, his long fair hair falling over his collar.

Quentin watched them ride slowly from his left to his right past the bottom of the hill. Justine appeared to be listening to Gavin, deferring to him as she nodded while saying very little herself. Certainly not the way she behaved with him! Quentin told himself.

Arriving at a crossroads, they reined in their horses and paused to sit side by side as they went on with what seemed to a discomfited Quentin to be an endless tête-à-tête.

At last Gavin Spencer rode off in the direction of

Prospect Hall, only to stop at the top of a small rise to turn and raise his hand in a farewell salute. Justine, who had been watching him, waved back until he was out of her sight. Then, rather than riding toward Round Hill, she swung her grey about and started slowly in the direction of the Manor.

Let her go, Quentin told himself. Retrieving his spyglass from the cleft in the rock, he returned to his stallion, fully intending to guide Lancelot not toward the Manor but in quite another direction. He started riding leisurely down the hill but when he came to the first turning he swung his mount to the left and spurred him ahead. Reaching level ground he galloped in the direction of the Manor until, seeing Justine a short distance ahead, he abruptly slowed to a canter to avoid the appearance of being in eager pursuit of her.

Justine had heard the staccato beat of hooves behind her and glanced over her shoulder, suppressing a sudden gasp when she saw Quentin galloping toward her. Do our paths cross by chance or by design? she asked herself when Quentin slowed his pace.

"A fine morning, Miss Riggs," he said, bringing his stallion alongside her bay and touching his riding crop to his hat.

"It is indeed, Lord Devon." She congratulated herself on her success in keeping her voice every bit as level as his.

"I consider this a lovely day for an early morning ride, Miss Riggs."

"I agree."

They rode for a time in an uneasy silence. "A few minutes ago I happened to observe Mr. Spencer,"

Quentin said in an elaborately casual way, "riding toward Prospect Hall."

"I fail to find that in the least surprising since I believe he resides there."

Is that what brought Quentin here this morning? she wondered. Did he consider Gavin Spencer as another challenge? Men seemed to thrive on challenges, they doted on competing with one another whether with their fists, their horses, at the gaming tables or with weapons on the battlefield. And she understood, at least in part, because her father had always been one to rise to challenges. And what of herself? she wondered.

Quentin reined in his black stallion. When she ignored this invitation to stop, and rode on, he again brought his horse alongside hers, and reached over and grasped her reins. Glaring at him, she was starting to protest when he said, "You went riding with Gavin Spencer this morning. With a man you scarcely know."

Taken aback by his accusing tone, she asked, "Is it possible, Lord Devon, that a court of chancery has, without my knowledge, named you my guardian?"

"If I were ever offered such an honor, I would hasten to decline. I have no desire to be responsible for a young lady so careless of her reputation."

How patronizing he was! "By riding with Mr. Gavin Spencer? How absurd! The gentleman in question was recommended to me on very good authority as being quite out-of-the-ordinary, a man of great courage and daring, a nonpareil."

"And who, pray tell, was this good authority?"

She allowed herself a self-satisfied smile. "The

best possible, at least I expect you would consider him so, since those words of commendation happen to be yours, Lord Devon, spoken in a conversation you held with Mr. Kinsdale."

He glowered at her. All at once he released her reins and, dusting his hands, said, "I wash my hands of you, Miss Riggs, once and for all." With that pronouncement he swung his horse away from her and rode ahead along the lane toward the Manor.

She gave a deep sigh of satisfaction as she watched him ride off. Good, she had bested him once and for all and, better still, in a few moments he would be gone from her sight; in all likelihood he was riding out of her life forever. Now, at long last, she told herself with a vigorous nod, she could forget Quentin Fletcher.

"Wait!" The cry burst from her lips, startling her by its fervor. Sometimes she failed to understand herself. Why, if she was so delighted by his departure, was she calling him back? And what did she mean to do or say if he heeded her cry?

When Quentin swung around in the saddle, Justine looked frantically around her and saw, across the fields, a lone oak perhaps half a mile away. Inspiration struck. "A race to the oak," she called and, without waiting for his reply, swung her bay from the lane and urged him toward the distant tree.

At first she was unable to tell whether he had accepted her challenge but then she heard hoofbeats behind her and, glancing over her shoulder, saw him leaning forward in the saddle, his riding crop raised. A quiver of excitement ran up and down her spine, the thrill of the race, the pursuit. And something more.

They pounded across the open field, Justine holding her lead. She had started with an advantage of several lengths which, she told herself, was fair since she rode sidesaddle while Quentin rode astride.

Seeing a double fence ahead, she slapped her bay's flank and he leaped high, easily clearing both top rails and recovering without losing stride. He galloped across a lush meadow, leaped a small stream bordered by weeping willows. Looking up she saw the oak looming ahead of her at the top of a low hill.

The pounding hoofbeats of Quentin's black grew louder. She glanced at him as he drew even and, when his black stallion edged ahead, Quentin's gaze met hers, the glint of sunlight reflecting from his eyes, and then he pulled away, increasing his lead with every stride, reaching the oak in time to rein in his perspiring horse and bring him around to face her as she cantered toward him, nodding to acknowledge his victory. Strangely enough, rather than being disappointed by her failure to win, she felt a throb of eager anticipation.

Without a word he swung to the ground, taking the reins of both horses and walking them for a time before leading them down the hill toward the willow trees bordering the stream in the meadow. When he reached the water, he let the horses drink while he walked to stand below her, raising his arms. She hesitated an instant before sliding down to him, his hands grasping her about the waist as he set her firmly on the ground and released her.

"A forfeit," he said, his voice strangely husky, "the loser must pay a forfeit."

Her heart skipped a beat. Quentin stood only a

breath away, his eyes dark, hooded, dangerous. His hands were at his sides, waiting for her to come into his arms, waiting to enfold her, waiting to hold her close. His lips were slightly parted, ready to greet her lips in a demanding, passionate kiss.

"A forfeit?" She whispered the question even though she knew full well what he meant.

Quentin said nothing, ignoring her words, seeming to read the truth of her fearful desire in her eyes. He reached to her, the fingers of one hand first caressing her cheek and then tilting her chin upward.

She saw sudden movement in the distance beyond him. Stepping back, she whispered, "Lord Alton."

Quentin stared at her, annoyed and confused. "Alton?" he repeated.

"And another gentleman from the eclipse party. On the road to Round Hill."

Quentin turned and watched the two horsemen who, though still a considerable distance away, were riding toward them. He stepped quickly to one of the willows and parted the hanging fronds as though drawing a curtain aside, inviting her to enter the shadowed circle beneath the tree. Once she was inside the cocoon of concealing branches, she realized they could see Lord Alton while remaining hidden from his view. Even their two horses, now grazing beside the brook, were, fortunately, concealed by the willows.

Lord Alton and his companion, deep in conversation, drew nearer and then nearer still. The road veered away from the meadow and the two riders followed it. Justine let out her breath in a sigh of relief.

She and Quentin were, she saw, enclosed in a twilight land, hidden from the inquisitive eyes of the world by an undulating green veil, the only sounds the sibilant murmur of the brook and a faint distant humming of bees. The air was soft and warm, a breeze rustling the willow fronds brought with it the sweet summer scents of wildflowers blooming in sun-drenched fields.

Quentin touched her arm, his fingers gentle, and she turned to him.

"Alton's gone," he said. "You have nothing to fear now."

Justine frowned. She had been afraid of discovery, she admitted to herself. Even though she had nothing to hide, had committed no indiscretion, she had been fearful that Lord Altop would find her with Quentin and, suspecting a rendezvous, use his newfound knowledge in some mean-spirited way. She did not trust the man.

She walked away from Quentin to the willow curtain, grasping one of the fronds, biting her lip as she idly twisted it around her hand. How she despised furtiveness! Though she had to admit she still longed for Quentin's embrace and for his kiss, she must not give way to temptation. She refused to live a clandestine life, hiding a secret love from the eyes of the world.

"Justine?" Quentin came to stand behind her.

She held, her heart pounding. If she turned to him, she would be lost. And, she admitted to herself, she wanted to be lost, wanted to be swept up into his arms, to feel his lips on hers. She was tempted by the chance to risk all, exhilarated by the hint of danger.

She started to turn to him, hesitated, and then shook

her head. What could she have been thinking? Had she completely lost her senses?

Releasing the willow strand, she pushed the fronds aside and stepped from the shadow of the sheltering tree, blinking in the sunlight as she walked hurriedly to the horses. She heard Quentin behind her and she turned to him—it was safe now to turn to him—and saw him start to speak but, as though sensing their moment had passed, he said nothing.

As they rode back to the Manor, saying little, Justine realized how afraid she had been, afraid not of Quentin nor of discovery by Lord Alton but afraid of her own undefined, tumultuous feelings and where, unbridled, they might lead her. Even so, and despite herself, she barely suppressed a sigh of regret. She had missed something, she felt with a searing ache of loss, a chance that would never come her way again.

She glanced to one side at Quentin but, finding him intently watching her, looked quickly away. How close to the precipice she had ventured! But now she was safe, the danger avoided, the temptation recognized and conquered. There were other men in the world besides Quentin Fletcher, amiable men, suitable men, men prepared to love and to cherish a woman rather than to challenge her. Gentle men.

Men such as Mr. Gavin Spencer of Prospect Hall.

Twelve

Early the following afternoon, Justine joined Prudence and Daphne for tea on the Manor terrace. It was a perfect summer day, a day of sun and shadow, of soft breezes and the sweet scent of flowers, all accompanied by the singing of birds.

"And did you enjoy Mr. Spencer's book?" Prudence asked as Justine stirred sugar into her tea.

Justine smiled at her. "Immensely. It was close on to one in the morning before I finished it."

"The book," Prudence explained to Daphne, "was Mr. Spencer's narrative recounting his adventures in the land of the czars."

"Not only is Gavin Spencer an intrepid explorer," Justine said with enthusiasm, "but he writes with a quite unexpected flair. I shivered with fear for his safety when a pack of wolves pursued his sled during a blizzard on the steppes."

"How terribly exciting," Daphne said, "and how fortunate Mr. Spencer survived. Otherwise we should have been denied the delightful anticipation of attending the costume ball at Prospect Hall which will give

167

all of us, but particularly Justine, the opportunity to become better acquainted with him. Was the ball his idea, I wonder, or might it have been his mother's inspiration?"

"I may be mistaken," Prudence said, "but I do suspect the notion came to Mr. Spencer on the spur of the moment. *After* he met you in the music room, Justine."

Was it possible, Justine asked herself, that Mr. Spencer had suggested the ball because of her? The idea, though appealing, struck her as being highly unlikely. "I imagine he wishes to become better acquainted with everyone staying at the Manor," she said.

Prudence shook her head. "That may well be true, but yesterday Mr. Spencer went riding with you, Justine, and not with any of the rest of us."

"I do hope nothing goes awry at the ball," Daphne said with a covert glance at Justine. Turning to Prudence, she asked, "When will Rodgers and Mrs. Hoskins travel to town to fetch material for the costumes?"

"They depart later this afternoon so I really must decide who I shall be. What person, either real or a figment of my imagination, either living or dead, do I admire the most? If only dear Eustace were here to advise me."

"I shall be Cleopatra," Daphne said, "a woman who changed the course of history."

"Lord Devon should have no problem choosing the person he most admires," Justine said caustically. "He will undoubtedly decide to come as himself."

Daphne gave her a speculative glance over the rim of her teacup but said nothing.

"Have *you* decided who you shall be, Justine?" Prudence asked.

Justine, expecting the others to be dismayed by her choice, raised her chin before she answered. "I intend to go to the ball as Robin Hood."

Both women stared at her. "But Justine," Prudence said, "Robin Hood was a man."

She had given up more than enough in the last few days, Justine told herself. On the matter of the costume, *her* costume, her mind was made up and she had no intention of retreating. "Or so we have always been taught to believe," she said, attempting to deflect further objections with a light touch. "Did it ever occur to you that someone named Robin could very easily have been a woman?"

"Robin Hood a woman?" Prudence seemed confused as she considered the notion. "Someone who lived in the depths of the forest and robbed wayfarers? And became romantically involved with Maid Marian?"

"I do believe," Daphne said, "that Justine is funning us since there happens to be little doubt Robin Hood was a man." She pursed her lips. "The costume could be quite charming," she admitted, "all in browns and greens with a long tunic and a belt to emphasize her narrow waist. And a hat with a feather. And boots."

"Not merely a tunic," Prudence insisted, "but leggings as well. But whether Justine's costume is charming or not, however, the notion is quite outside of enough. Not only her coming to the ball costumed as a man but a lawless one at that."

"Not exactly lawless," Justine pointed out, "since Robin Hood stole from the rich to help the poor."

Prudence sighed. "But my dear girl, you seem to forget that *we* would be considered to be among the rich."

"The costume," Daphne said, "could be quite pleasantly revealing with all the advantages of dampened muslins without having to resort to such an outrageous subterfuge."

"When we passed through the wood on our ride to Round Hill yesterday morning," Justine told them, "Mr. Spencer expressed a great admiration for Robin Hood and his daring exploits. His comments gave me the idea."

"While Mr. Spencer may admire Robin Hood," Prudence said rather tartly, "you may be certain he would never consider marrying him." She threw up her hands. "However, if you wish to go to the ball as Robin Hood, I will have nothing further to say on the subject. When I was a young lady—" She shook her head, sighed, and, seemingly recalling her promise, said no more.

As they sat for a time without speaking, eating scones and sipping tea, Justine gradually became aware of a heightening of her senses, a quickening of her pulses. She had the eerie feeling that someone was watching her. Turning slightly toward Daphne, she glanced from the corner of her eye in the direction of the house. At first she saw nothing except the reflection of the lowering sun glinting from the windows but then, her gaze going to one of the upper windows overlooking the terrace, she drew in a quick breath

170

when she caught sight of the dark figure of a man staring down at them, at her.

Quentin.

She should ignore him, she told herself even as she went on surreptitiously watching him. Was he gazing idly from the window, she wondered, or was he looking at her? And what were his thoughts at this moment? She would, she supposed, never know.

When she saw Quentin release the curtain and step back from the window, Justine sighed in disappointment but then shook her head. She had put Quentin behind her; now she must look ahead to the pleasures of the costume ball, she counseled herself, to the music and the dancing, to conversation with amiable gentlemen and, perhaps, to a furthering of her acquaintance with Mr. Gavin Spencer . . .

Hearing a tapping at the door behind him, Quentin let the curtain fall and reluctantly turned from the window.

"You asked to see me, my lord?" Rodgers said as he entered the sitting room.

Quentin nodded. "About the damn costume, for a start. I believe I shall appear at Spencer's ball as a highwayman. Will you see what you can unearth in London to outfit me?"

"Of course, my lord, and, if I may say so, a highwayman is an excellent choice. I picture you as a clever, dashing, mysterious, well-born romantic rogue who has been forced to temporarily descend into a life of crime by the evil machinations of his enemies."

What a vivid imagination the man had, Quentin thought, immediately going on to say, "A highwayman was my second choice, you understand. It so hap-

171

pens that Gerard Kinsdale has opted to appear as the gentleman I hold in highest esteem."

"Mr. Benjamin Franklin, the American of many talents? I am surprised that he would be your first choice."

Ah. It wasn't often, Quentin felt, that anyone succeeded in surprising Rodgers. "What of you, Rodgers?" he asked. "If you were to attend this costume ball, who would you choose to be?"

Rodgers frowned in thought. "I hesitate to say for fear of sounding presumptuous, of having aspirations above and beyond my station, but I would appear as Mr. William Shakespeare of Stratford."

"Ah, yes." How like Rodgers. "And Miss Riggs," Quentin asked as casually as he could, "what costume has Miss Riggs selected?"

"If her choice were not already common knowledge among the ladies, I would have to refrain from revealing her decision. She insists on appearing as a character somewhat akin to your own. She intends to appear as none other than the legendary Robin Hood."

Quentin raised his eyebrows, frowned, then laughed in delight, striking his palm with his fist. "My God," he said, "I admire her spirit. She refuses to turn back, even though warned she may be drifting toward a waterfall as high as Niagara." He walked to the window and glanced down at Justine. "I can almost hear her suggesting," he said, more to himself than to Rodgers, "that Robin Hood might very well have been a woman."

"A most unlikely possibility," Rodgers interposed.

"And," Quentin went on, "speculating that if I were

172

to come to the ball as the gentleman I most admired I would come as myself." Again turning to Rodgers, he said, "Confound it, Rodgers, I could be completely mistaken but now and again I have this strange feeling I can read her thoughts."

"If one actually had the ability to know what our supposed friends thought of us, our discoveries would undoubtedly be both surprising and unsettling. And, as a result, the number of our friends would most likely decrease."

"And," Quentin said, "if we knew what our servants really thought of us, the ranks of the unemployed would increase—" He broke off. "To the business at hand," he said. "What information have you gleaned regarding Mr. Gavin Spencer?"

"Surprisingly little, my lord, since the help at Prospect Hall proved to be remarkably close-mouthed on the subject, suspiciously so, although they all speak highly of the splendid Mr. Spencer but in the most general terms. Their reticence almost makes me wonder if they have something to hide."

"You might have better results if a few pounds sterling were to change hands."

"Perhaps, but I have my doubts." Rodgers paused. "Have you ever heard of a widowed lady from London by the name of Mallory, my lord? Mrs. Alicia Mallory?"

"The name means nothing to me. Who is this Alicia Mallory?"

"That, it seems, is something of a puzzle. From what I gather, there is a certain pattern followed by this Mrs. Mallory and Mr. Spencer. Shortly after Mr. Spencer returns from one of his expeditions, Mrs.

Mallory makes her appearance at Prospect Hall and takes up residence in spacious though remote quarters in the west wing of the house. What she does there is a mystery to one and all. She takes her meals in her rooms, behaves rather furtively and is seldom seen by any of the servants. Although Mr. Spencer visits her regularly and spends considerable time with her, there is no evidence of their having any sort of romantic involvement or even of their being friends. In truth, Mr. Spencer is said to resent the presence of Mrs. Mallory."

"And yet Spencer spends time with her and continues to invite her to his home."

"Exactly, my lord. A daft business but one that may well have a simple explanation. I intend to persist in my inquiries while in London, both regarding this mysterious visitor to Prospect Hall and Mr. Spencer himself."

"Capital," Quentin said. *Alicia Mallory.* He repeated the name as he promised himself that he would do whatever he could to uncover her secret. "Both of us must do all in our power," he told Rodgers, "to assist Mr. Kinsdale and Mrs. Baldwin in their search for an appropriate suitor for Miss Riggs."

Rodgers inclined his head, then glanced toward the clock on the mantel.

"I shall delay you no longer," Quentin told him. "I wish you godspeed on your journey to London."

He would do his utmost, Quentin told himself as he watched Rodgers leave, to make certain Justine was suitably wed. His concern for her welfare, he told himself with a certain satisfaction, was completely unselfish. She might be a perverse and combative young lady, she might be naive and poorly tutored in feminine skills, but despite all of these deficiencies he nevertheless felt a gentleman's obligation to look after her.

His feeling for her was akin to the concern of a brother for a sister, a younger sister. Yes, that was the truth of the matter, Justine Riggs was an unfortunate, dowerless orphan who needed the protection and help of an older man, his protection and his help. She required the guidance of a man of the world and who was better qualified than himself to provide that guidance? There were more than a few rakes and roués in the *ton* who would not hesitate to employ deceit and trickery to take advantage of an attractive young girl from the country.

The predatory Lord Alton, for one, who was all the more dangerous for coming wrapped, as the saying went, in clean sheets. He must, Quentin warned himself, be careful not to underestimate Alton; the man not only considered himself irresistible to the ladies, he would go to almost any lengths to have his way with them, particularly if in so doing he could discomfit Quentin Fletcher.

Quentin returned to the window once more and looked down at Justine. To his surprise, his heart lurched at the sight of her. How tremendously appealing he found the dark sheen of her curling hair, the bloom in her cheeks, the tilt of her nose and the soft curves of her body. All at once he sensed, without knowing why but with great certainty, that she and Prudence—Daphne was no longer with them—were talking about him. If only he were close enough to overhear them but, alas, he was not . . .

"I was amazed when Lord Devon accepted the invitation to the Spencer masquerade," Prudence was saying, "since he will now have to remain at the Manor another fortnight. He rarely stays more than a few days at a house party before becoming frightfully bored."

Justine nodded but made no reply.

"At times, Justine," Prudence went on, "you appear to detest Lord Devon to such a degree that I wonder whether you might secretly favor him."

"I have never encountered anyone quite like him before," Justine admitted. "I suppose I find myself fascinated by him just as someone else might be fascinated by a zebra or a giraffe on exhibit in a menagerie."

"To my way of thinking," Prudence said, "Lord Devon more closely resembles a tawny lion, the king of beasts, rather than a zebra or giraffe. And Gavin Spencer, what animal does he remind one of? A magnificent stag, perhaps. But why are we comparing gentlemen to animals?"

"Could it be because so many of them perceive us as their prey, as weak and docile victims to be pursued, captured by means of traps and ruses and then carried home where we become their prisoners for life?"

"Do you actually believe our plight is so dire?" Prudence wanted to know. "Surely not."

Justine sighed and shook her head. "No," she conceded, "but what I do believe, or have come to believe, is that women should value their senses over sensibilities. Not all women—how can I speak for so many others?—but myself. I should begin listening to my head rather than my heart."

Prudence stared at her. "Has something happened in the last few days?" she asked at last. "You seem so different to me."

"I admit I have changed." Justine looked down the slope of the lawn to the gazebo and beyond to where the shadows of the clouds drifted across the folds of the hills and valleys. "When I first came to London I believed I should follow my heart, that I would somehow instinctively know what was the right thing to do." She shook her head. "I no longer believe I know."

"In choosing a husband, at least," Prudence said, "the heart can prove to be a treacherous guide."

"I agree. The decision is too important to be left to the vagaries of our emotions. Suitability, compatibility and amiability are much more important than the fact that a man's look or smile or touch is able to make your heart beat a trifle faster than it ever did before."

"Louis Nannini," Prudence said.

"I beg your pardon?"

"I spoke without thinking." Prudence smiled wistfully. "Louis Nannini was a gentleman I once knew, a gentleman I haven't thought of in years and years. No, I fear I exaggerate, he has crossed my mind now and again. I often wonder what ever became of Louis Nannini."

"An Italian gentleman?" Justine asked, intrigued. She had always assumed there had been but one man in Prudence's life. The revered Eustace.

Prudence nodded. "I was considered quite pretty when I was young," she said, "being petite with blond hair and, as you can see, blue eyes."

"Sometimes they seem a dark, dark blue, at other times light as a cornflower."

"Louis Nannini thought they were the loveliest eyes he had ever seen, or so he told me." Prudence blushed slightly. "It was all very romantic. He was a northern Italian, from a small town in Tuscany, very dark and very handsome and extremely charming. He told me he loved me and, for a time, I was convinced I loved him."

"I never heard you speak of him before."

"It all came to naught, of course, since he was only a riding instructor, a man without money who lived mainly by his wits. When my mother found one of his letters—he wrote the most wonderfully amorous letters—my father sent me away for a long visit with my aunt Elizabeth near Paisley in Scotland. When my father finally allowed me to return to London, I discovered that Mr. Nannini had married in secret and emigrated to Canada. Not more than six months later, I married Eustace Baldwin. I often wonder what became of Louis Nannini."

How sad! was Justine's initial reaction but, on reflection, she realized that Prudence's situation was, in some respects, akin to her own. "You may not have thought so at the time," she said, "but you were fortunate to have been sent away. Otherwise you might never have met Eustace and I know how devoted to him you were."

Prudence stood and walked to the stone wall at the edge of the terrace where she stood staring into the far distance, almost as though, Justine thought, she was able to look into the past.

"Fortunate?" Prudence repeated. "At the time, of

course, I was heartbroken. I cried all the way to Scotland. I often wonder what would have happened if I had possessed more courage—" She stopped and Justine thought she heard her sigh softly.

"Yes," Prudence said, "as you say, I was fortunate." She dabbed at her face with a lace handkerchief but when she turned to Justine there were no signs of tears on her face. "I did love Eustace," she said. "Over the years I learned to appreciate his kindness and his patience."

"Everyone has told me how devastated you were by his death."

Prudence frowned. "It never occurred to me before this moment," she said, "but now I wonder if, after Eustace died, I tried to give him all the love I might have withheld while he lived." She shook her head. "No, what a strange notion, I loved Eustace dearly and always will. I *was* fortunate to have him, so very fortunate, I should count my blessings."

"Just as I," Justine said, "should count mine."

And, she reminded herself, she had been blessed in many ways. She had found a friend and protector in Prudence Baldwin, the woman who had given her a new life in London; she had realized the folly of her infatuation with Quentin before it was too late; she had the excitement of the costume ball to look forward to and the likelihood that she would become better acquainted with Gavin Spencer, a man well worth any young lady's interest.

Why, then, she wondered, when she had so much to be thankful for, did she feel this unease, this sense of wrongness?

Thirteen

The carriage stopped, and Justine stepped down to the walkway pausing to look up at the twin columns framing the entrance to the Spencer country house and, beyond, the windows ablaze with lights.

"Prospect Hall!" Daphne murmured from behind her.

The night of the costume ball had arrived at last. A new page was being turned in her life, Justine thought. This was the start of another chapter.

Gavin Spencer, tall, poised and imposing in the flowing white burnoose of an Arab sheik, greeted them in a reception room between the entryway of Prospect Hall and the grand ballroom, telling them that his mother was, unfortunately, slightly indisposed but hoped to join them later. He bowed over the hands of Daphne, a veiled Cleopatra whose tight-fitting patterned tunic had straps that barely succeeded in covering her breasts, and Prudence, who had at the last minute decided to come as Caesar's wife, her costume a stola, the long draped robe favored by Roman women.

Justine was unsure whether Prudence had selected the Roman costume so she could serve as a sedate foil for Cleopatra, the temptress, or whether thinking about her long-lost love, Louis Nannini, had given her the idea of dressing as someone who might have been one of his remote ancestors.

When Gavin Spencer, who wore no mask, welcomed Justine to his home, he raised her hand to his lips and then, rather than releasing it at once, allowed his grasp to linger. As his gaze also lingered, his eyes roaming in evident admiration from her close-cropped black curls beneath a forest-green feathered hat, to her domino mask, to her long green tunic with its jagged hemline, to the quiver of feather-tipped arrows slung on her back, and finally down to her form-fitting green leggings.

"I *do* like your costume," he said, releasing her hand. "I find it demure and yet so very provocative. I especially admire a woman who dares to dress as a man."

Justine nodded to acknowledge the compliment. If this had been Quentin greeting her, she realized, she would have made a spirited answer, challenging him in some manner. In a perverse way, she felt disappointed at not having the opportunity.

Gavin bowed to Gerard, dressed as the American, Benjamin Franklin, and to Ogden, who had stubbornly refused to appear as anyone but himself.

When she entered the ballroom, Justine frowned in surprise. She had expected the unusual from Gavin Spencer who was, after all, a world-traveler, an adventurer, a man who reveled in taking enormous risks. The ballroom, however, was perfectly ordinary—if a ballroom in a great English country house could ever be considered ordinary. The spacious room was lit by candles in circled tiers on two chandeliers, its walls were festooned with fresh roses, and the dancers were reflected from a large gilt-framed mirror above the marble fireplace.

As they made their way through the crush at the side of the dance floor, Justine glanced about her, smiling at the sight of kings cavorting with courtesans, Crusaders dancing with Greek goddesses, gypsies beguiling military heroes (she counted at least three General Wellingtons), and a queen talking earnestly to a red Indian wearing a feathered war bonnet.

Quentin, as best she could tell, was not in the room.

After dancing a country set with John Willoughby—"I expected to be the only Iron Duke," he told her in a tone of resigned disgust—she was sitting chatting with Daphne and Ogden when she noticed Lord Alton, costumed as the German general, Blücher—a generous moustache added to his upper lip, a medal-laden red ribbon sweeping diagonally across his chest and a sword at his side—threading between dancers.

"How handsome he is!" Daphne murmured. "How virile! He reminds me of a proud young god come from Valhalla to walk the Earth."

"Lord Alton?" Justine asked in surprise.

"No, no, certainly not. Mr. Gavin Spencer." She sighed. "Ah, if only I were a few years younger."

Justine turned in the direction of Daphne's glance to find Gavin striding toward them, his white robes flowing behind.

Ogden scarcely had time to utter a disparaging harrumph before Gavin joined them. "Miss Riggs," he said, bowing over her hand, "may I have the pleasure of your company?"

Justine, pleased and flattered, conscious of the envious glances of the other women, nodded and, rising, took his arm, feeling petite beside him. She expected him to lead her to the dance floor where another set was forming but instead he asked, "Would you enjoy seeing a bit more of Prospect Hall? I find this constant nattering quite exhausting."

When she nodded, he led her away from the dancers to an alcove at the far end of the ballroom. Opening a small unobtrusive door, he ushered her through an anteroom into a corridor lit by candles in sconces along both walls.

"Despite the chatter," he said, "I so enjoy masked balls. All of us wear masks of one sort or another during every day of our lives, trying to pretend we're something other than we actually are. At least at a masquerade we can be honest about our deception."

"All of us wear masks?" she asked. "I never thought I attempted to hide my true self."

Did she? Justine wondered.

"Possibly not, but if so, you, Miss Riggs, are a most unusual young woman. Most of us have secrets either large or small that we wish to conceal from the world, secrets concealed by veils that we shed only reluctantly. How dull and prosaic we would be without our secrets."

She started to protest, to inform him that she had no secrets either large or small, but she suddenly realized she would be telling an untruth. Her deep feeling for Quentin, even though now a thing of the past, was a secret, her never-to-be-revealed secret.

"Another reason I enjoy masquerades," Gavin said, "is the opportunity they give me to discover some of the more lurid fantasies of my guests. The timid gentlemen, for instance, who dream of being kings or generals, the sedate women who picture themselves as seductive temptresses."

"And what of you, Mr. Spencer, who chose to be a sheik."

"Call me Gavin, please," he said, smiling down at her. "Will you, Justine?"

Her nod was rewarded with another warming smile. "To me," he said as he led her along the corridor, "a sheik, that rider of the desert sands, is a man free of the constraints of stodgy, so-called civilized countries such as England. A sheik, at least this one, rides where he chooses, when he chooses, associating with whomever he wishes, with none of the scandal-mongers of the *ton* watching and weighing his every move in hopes of witnessing a misstep that will allow them to call down the wrath of society on his head."

Justine nodded; his words struck a responsive chord. Evidently she and Gavin Spencer had more than a little in common for she, too, had felt the unease of being under the disapproving scrutiny of those around her.

Hearing the faint throb of drums coming from behind a closed door a short distance ahead, she looked questioningly up at him.

After a moment's hesitation, he said, "An exotic entertainment from the eastern shores of the Mediterranean for a few of my more sophisticated guests.

Nothing really shocking, I assure you," he added hastily, "merely a trifle unconventional."

"More than a few people," she told him, "have accused me of being unconventional."

"This, however," he said with a smile—he had, she told herself, a most engaging smile—"is entertainment more to the tastes of my gentlemen guests rather than the ladies."

He started to lead her away when the door of the room opened and one of the Wellingtons emerged. In the few moments before the general closed the door behind him, Justine caught a whiff of the spicy aroma of incense mingled with the smoke of cigars and—although the room was lit only by a few gaudy Chinese lanterns—a brief glimpse of Gavin Spencer's "exotic entertainment."

The guests, mostly men, were seated on oversized cushions along all sides of the room. To the right, a drummer sat cross-legged on the floor, his bare upper torso gleaming a satiny black in the muted light. In the center of the room a woman with hair of jet and skin of copper, her feet bare, her lithe body swathed in flowing diaphanous veils, danced to the rhythmic beat of the drums, a sinuous dance that promised— what? Justine felt she would rather not try to guess.

Even after the door closed, her skin prickled with uneasiness. She sensed an almost tangible presence of something alien and forbidden, but she could not tell whether this otherness came from the heady scent, from the arousing throb of the drums, from the otherworldly light of the lanterns, or from some other source entirely. Whatever the strangeness was, it seemed to be communicated to her not by one of her five senses but by some sixth sense.

She gave a start when a hand gripped her arm. Without a word of explanation, Gavin hurried her along the hallway. When she glanced up she found him looking at her as though gauging her response to what she had seen.

"I promised to show you Prospect Hall," Gavin said, his voice studiedly casual, "and I shall."

She frowned but said nothing. Why had he taken her near that room? she wondered. Had it been inadvertent or by design? Was he testing her in some way, judging her response to the out-of-the-ordinary? Perhaps he wanted to reveal something of himself to her, give her a hint of one aspect of his life. She would, Justine decided, bide her time before asking him his reasons, since her own reaction to what she had seen, her own thoughts, were hopelessly jumbled. Was it possible to be fascinated and yet repelled at the same time? Might she be, after all, the naive country girl Quentin claimed her to be?

She let him lead her to where the corridor ended in a spacious, high-ceilinged hallway. Directly in front of her she saw a staircase rising half a story before turning sharply to the left and disappearing into darkness.

"These stairs lead to the west wing," Gavin said as he turned away, his hand firm under her arm. "Prospect Hall is much too immense for the two of us, my mother and myself, so, shortly after my father died, we closed the west wing."

As she passed under an archway to leave the hall, Justine glanced back, thinking she had glimpsed

186

movement at the top of the stairs. Now, however, there was only the darkness . . .

When he looked down from the top of the stairs and quite unexpectedly saw Justine with Gavin Spencer, Quentin cursed angrily under his breath. He so forgot himself that he hesitated before stepping away from the newel post into the concealing darkness. When Justine glanced back toward him, he wondered if he had waited too long but when she gave no sign she had seen him, walking on and disappearing from his view, he assumed that his highwayman's black capes, hat and mask had allowed him to blend in with the shadows of the upper hall.

Quentin shook his head, unable to understand the ferocity of his sudden anger. He was being petty and mean-spirited, especially since he wanted Gavin Spencer to take an interest in Justine; he meant to encourage him as long as he, Quentin, was convinced of the other man's sincerity.

Which was why, against his better judgment, he was skulking about here in the west wing of Prospect Hall. He disliked what he was doing for he had never pictured himself as a stealthy intruder who furtively made his way into the upper reaches of another man's home, but tonight that was precisely what he had done.

He was here because Rodgers, despite making inquiries during his trip to town, had failed to discover any clues as to the identity of Mrs. Alicia Mallory, the mysterious woman who had supposedly taken up residence in the west wing of Prospect Hall where she and Gavin Spencer—did what? Quentin had not the slightest inkling. He was, however, determined to discover the truth before the evening was over.

He walked cautiously along the unlighted, musty hall with his right hand now and again touching the near wall to keep himself from losing his way. He ignored a distant creaking as the old house settled; he shrugged off scurrying sounds nearby, telling himself they were undoubtedly made by mice in the walls.

Reaching once more toward the wall, he groped in vain as his hand encountered—nothing at all. He must, he realized, have come to a turn in the hallway. Peering to his right he saw a thin horizontal line of light coming, he supposed, from beneath a door. Rodgers had been right, as he invariably was, someone did live in the west wing. Could it be Mrs. Mallory?

Walking ahead with more assurance, Quentin approached the door to the lighted room only to hesitate when he reached it as, momentarily, his misgivings returned. He was doing this for Justine, he reassured himself, to protect her from making a possibly grievous mistake. If Gavin Spencer led a secret life, and Quentin had always believed him too good to be true, then this room might very well reveal the nature of that secret.

He lifted the latch, pushed and felt the door swing inward. Narrowing his eyes and peering into the dimly lit, sparsely furnished room, he saw a woman, her greying hair gathered in a bun at the back of her head, sitting at a desk reading by the light of two candles.

At first she failed to see him but then, as though sensing his presence, she gave him a startled stare and opened her mouth as though to scream.

"I beg your pardon," Quentin said, raising his hands to try to tell her he meant no harm. Realizing he still wore his highwayman's mask, he hastily removed it. "The costume ball," he explained. "Could you kindly direct me to the ballroom?"

The woman rose warily from her chair.

"Do you happen to be Mrs. Alicia Mallory?" Quentin asked.

"Yes, I'm Mrs. Mallory," she said cautiously.

"How extraordinary." After taking a step into the room, Quentin stopped to glance down at her cluttered desk. A suspicion began to take shape in his mind. "I have heard so much about you," he said. "In London."

"You have?" Mrs. Mallory's voice showed she was both pleased and suspicious.

"And about your wonderful work," Quentin went on, stepping even closer to the desk as he wondered precisely what the nature of that work might be.

"I never dreamed," Mrs. Mallory said, "that my fame, scant as it is, had spread beyond a small circle of friends."

"It has, I assure you." Quentin stepped to the desk, looked down at the papers there and smiled to himself. His suspicion had been correct. Now he understood why Mrs. Mallory was here at Prospect Hall and he knew the nature of her relationship with Gavin Spencer.

When, several minutes later, he left Mrs. Mallory's room in the west wing, he started toward the stairway intending to find Justine and reveal Gavin Spencer's secret. She should be immediately informed as to what sort of man this supposed paragon was. But wait. He stopped, scowling. Was that the honorable thing to do? This was not, certainly, a matter of life and death. Should he reveal what he had discovered by stealth when the other man's secret might have very little bearing on the desirability of Gavin Spencer as a suitor?

Damn. This *was* a dilemma.

Never one to vacillate, Quentin made up his mind. His lips must remain sealed. Gavin Spencer's secret would remain safe. For now, at least.

At that very moment, Gavin Spencer was showing Justine still another room in the sprawling labyrinth of rooms that comprised the east wing of Prospect Hall, rooms built as additions to the original house by his paternal grandfather, Hayden Spencer. This particular room was decorated in a style popular in the middle of the preceding century, the furniture all of mahogany, the legs of the desks and tables ending in ball-and-claw feet, the elaborate mirror featuring two candles in holders at its base.

As he led her from the room, Gavin said, "Will you accept my apology?"

She stared at him in confusion. "Apology?" she repeated.

"For taking you anywhere near that room where you saw the dancer."

"What I saw failed to shock me," Justine said. On the other hand, she admitted to herself, the sensuousness of the dance *had* disturbed her. Still, there *was* a difference in the two feelings, although only of degree.

"I view you, Justine," he said, "even after our admittedly brief acquaintance, as a very special young lady, one who is not only different but also rather extraordinary. I happen to consider myself different as well, and I say so not from pride but to make you aware of the truth, and so I may have been tempted, wrongfully tempted I now admit, to hide nothing from you, hoping you would come to accept me as I am."

His praise warmed her but made her ill at ease at the same time. Did he really know very much about her? She doubted that he did. And she was aware she knew even less about him.

Before she could reply—perhaps, she thought, so she would not have to reply—Gavin opened another door and stood aside so she could look past him at furniture fashioned in the Roman manner. One of the bookcases resembled the facade of a temple, a sideboard was covered with a marble top and a couch was shaped like a Roman bed.

"As you are probably aware," he told her, "this style was popular only fifteen years ago. My grandfather had the rather peculiar notion that he would never die as long as the Hall kept growing and so, as the years passed, he added one room after another. In the end, of course, his notion was proved wrong and he did pass on, but he lived well into his seventy-sixth year. There were those who considered him an eccentric and called this house his folly, but we in the family were rather proud of the old man."

What strange behavior, Justine thought. Recollecting that someone had described Gavin's father as "daft," she asked, "Did your father have the same notion about the house?"

"Not at all. As often happens with fathers and sons,

my father took quite the opposite tack. Soon after he inherited the Hall, all of his affairs went to the bad and, as he slipped into a decline, he began selling off his land acre by acre to meet his growing debts. He once told me he expected to live until the last parcel was sold but not one day more. He, like my grandfather, was proved wrong in the end since he had only disposed of a little more than half the estate by the time he died."

When Justine made no comment, Gavin said, "Happily, I inherited neither my grandfather's mania for building nor my father's need to sell."

Justine wondered whether his father's fecklessness had in some way led Gavin Spencer into his life of adventure. He had, perhaps, felt compelled to prove something to himself as well as to his family, felt a need to redeem his father's misspent life with one of achievement.

Gavin seemed so contradictory. An imposing figure of a man, tall and broad-shouldered, a man who had proved his courage time and time again, he was unfailingly courteous and surprisingly gentle. He did not seem to challenge her in any way; he harbored none of the threat of violence she at times detected in Quentin.

As they walked on in silence, the sound of the music became louder but when they came to the top of the staircase leading down to the ballroom, Justine held back. "Something puzzles me," she told him.

Gavin looked at her sharply, then smiled. "You have only to ask," he told her, "and I shall do my best to answer."

"A few days ago," she said, "I read your narrative

of your expedition's thrilling trek across Russian steppes. I enjoyed the book tremendously, especially the felicitous way you described your adventures in that alien land."

He sketched a bow.

"The style of writing in the book, though," she went on, "is nothing at all akin to the way you fashion your sentences when you speak. It never occurred to me before that the manner in which one writes, the cadences and the use of words, and the way one speaks might be completely different."

"I could tell you," he said, "that such a difference is very possible but I have a very good reason to want to be completely honest with you. Therefore I shall make my confession and throw myself on your mercy. In a sense I deceived you; I deceived everyone who read my books. You see, Justine, I never wrote them."

Fourteen

Taken aback, Justine said, "All the books describing your travels were actually written by someone else?"

"By a woman, it so happens," Gavin told her, "a widow named Mrs. Alicia Mallory. When I return from one of my journeys to a foreign land I give her my diaries and my journals to read and we discuss the events and decide what to include and what to leave out. She then proceeds to write a first draft of the book, I make whatever changes are necessary and she goes on to prepare the final version."

Justine shook her head in denial. "But your name is on the book as the author," she protested.

"If the book were published under Mrs. Mallory's name, as I must confess it rightfully should be, hardly anyone would buy a copy and so very few people would have the chance to learn about Russia, Egypt, Greece and Africa. I did write the narrative of my first journey to Switzerland but, alas, Mr. Cloverly and the other booksellers considered it quite unacceptable and therefore introduced me to Mrs. Mallory."

"I suppose not everyone has a narrative gift,"

Justine admitted, concealing her surprise and disappointment. "But then I also suppose that accomplishing something of significance in this world is more important than merely being able to write about it."

"I always believed so. Not that I begrudge Mrs. Mallory earning a fair recompense for the skill needed to turn my leaden words into gold."

"As far as we know from reading the Bible," Justine said, as she sought to convince herself that Gavin had done nothing dishonorable, "Jesus never wrote a word of the Gospels, never left any written record of his own. All we know of him was written by his disciples. Not," she hastened to add, "that I compare you to Him."

"Of course not." Gavin smiled slightly. "As I told you, I have one aim and one aim only, and that is to be completely honest with you. Otherwise I would have kept my little secret to myself."

He *had* mentioned having a secret, Justine recalled. Although dismayed to discover he was not the author of the books bearing his name, she told herself that his deception, while disappointing, was less than damning. And he had willingly, almost eagerly, revealed the truth.

"Before we return to the ballroom," he told her as he turned aside and opened a door opposite the top of the staircase, "I want to show you where my career, if career is the right word, had its beginnings."

Looking past him, she was surprised to see an ordinary chamber whose furniture was covered with Holland cloth. On the far side of the room, French doors led to a balcony overlooking the moonlit rear of the Hall.

"This was a box room when I was a boy," he said, "and we often played here, Clive Culver and I. How I hated Clive Culver. He was the son of a friend of my father, a big burly fellow who took delight in teasing me, in calling me names, in accusing me of being not only a coward but a mother's boy as well. He threatened to thrash me if I ever told anyone about his bullying."

Even as Justine admired his frankness, she had difficulty imagining Gavin Spencer being afraid of anyone or anything.

She followed him across the room where he opened the French doors and they stepped onto a small balcony enclosed by an iron railing. She saw an identical balcony close on fifteen feet away with doors leading to an adjoining room.

"One day," Gavin told her, "Clive and I were on this balcony when I boasted that I could leap from this railing to the next."

Leaning over the rail Justine looked down and, in the pale light from the moon, saw stone flagging far below. Shivering at the prospect of plunging to injury or possible death, she shook her head. "Did you really think you could leap that far?" she asked.

Gavin shrugged. "I had no idea whether I could or not but I was tired of being the butt of Clive's taunts. I might not be able to leap from railing to railing but at least I could try. Clive, of course, maintained that no one, boy or man, could leap that far and dared me to do try, hoping, I expect, that I would cry off and thus prove him right about my lack of courage."

Gathering his flowing white robe in one hand, Gavin climbed to the top of the rail. "He left me no choice but to make the attempt, or that was what I thought. How could I decline his challenge without branding myself a coward? I climbed up here, holding to the side of the house with one hand, afraid to look down, and belatedly realizing I could never jump that distance without a running start. And perhaps not even then."

"What did you do?" Justine asked.

"This." Gavin crouched on the rail.

Justine's hand flew to her mouth to stifle a gasp of horror as he suddenly leaped up and out toward the other rail. She knew with a fearful certainty he would never reach it, that he would fall to his death far below on the flagstones. How foolhardy to attempt such a dangerous leap!

She watched with disbelief when, instead of falling, he grasped the creeper vines growing up the side of the house, clutching them with the fingers of both hands while at the same time gaining a momentary toehold on the side of the house with his boots, scrabbling his way across the wall to drop safely onto the far railing.

Her knees went weak with relief when he swung down to the far balcony and turned toward her; involuntarily she clapped her hands in recognition of his feat.

Gavin acknowledged her applause with a bow. After brushing the leaves and dirt from his robes, he entered the adjoining room and she left the balcony, rejoining him in the hall.

"You frightened me," she told him as they started down the stairway.

"I was more than frightened the first time I made

the leap," he said, "I was absolutely terrified. Clive was suitably impressed, though, not only by my succeeding but because I dared to attempt the leap in the first place, something he would never have done. He never teased me after that day. And I realized I possessed a certain amount of bottom, of courage, that I dared to take calculated risks if the reward was great enough. And that is what I have been doing ever since."

"I think I must have been just as impressed tonight as Clive was years ago. You might have been killed or horribly hurt if you lost your grip on the vine."

"Death is a far better fate than being mocked and derided."

Not certain she agreed—death, after all, was so final—Justine glanced at him and realized he was quite sincere. She had to admit Gavin was a brave man—though perhaps a bit foolhardy.

As they entered the ballroom a footman approached Gavin, speaking softly to him, so softly she could not hear.

After the footman left, Gavin glanced around the room, as though to assure himself that his guests lacked nothing, and then turned to her.

"My mother is still indisposed," he said, "and has asked me to go to her in her chambers."

"Is she all right?" Justine asked, concern threading her voice.

"Oh, yes, she often takes to her bed for a day or two at a time after overtaxing herself, which, unfortunately, she did in making the preparations for tonight's ball. You may judge the state of her health for yourself since she requests you to accompany me if you will."

When Justine stared at him in surprise, Gavin added, "Two weeks ago, when I returned from the Manor after our morning ride, I told her about you. Ever since, she has plied me with questions, questions of the most friendly sort, I assure you."

With some misgivings, Justine glanced down at her tunic and leggings. "Will she object," she asked, "to seeing me garbed as Robin Hood?"

"Not at all. A costume worn to a masquerade ball means nothing to her."

Gavin offered her his arm and, after a moment's pause—was it really appropriate to meet his mother while costumed as a man? she wondered—she took it and let him escort her from the ballroom and across a parlor to stairs leading up to a wing of the Hall she had not yet visited.

"These are the family quarters," he told her.

When he tapped on a door near the top of the stairway, a woman's voice said, "Gavin?" He opened the door and, as he led an apprehensive Justine inside, she caught a whiff of lavender scent.

The wallpaper of the bedchamber was gold and cream, the furniture gracefully curved in the Louis XV style, the bed a four-poster in an alcove with an imposing dark blue canopy; the only light shone from a lamp on a table on the far side of the bed. Charlotte Spencer sat in bed propped up on pillows, her face in shadow. To Justine, she appeared unexpectedly youthful with ash-blond hair framing an oval, high-cheekboned face.

Gavin strode to the side of the bed where he knelt

beside his mother. She took his hand in both of hers and raised his fingers to her lips as she murmured soft words of endearment; Gavin lowered his head to her breast, creating, in Justine's view, a loving tableau of adoring mother and devoted son. At the same time she felt a pang for what had been denied her as a child, the tender care and the love of a mother.

At last Gavin rose and held out his hand to Justine who came into the alcove to stand at his side. "Mother," he said, "this is Miss Justine Riggs."

Taking Justine's hands in hers, Charlotte Spencer drew her to the bed, close enough to allow Justine to see that Mrs. Spencer owed much if not all of her youthful appearance to the shadows cast by the single lamp and to the liberal application of rouge and powder. Somehow the revelation saddened her. She was, though, relieved to see that her unorthodox costume did not seem to shock the other woman.

"My dear," Mrs. Spencer said, "how very lovely you are. I often accuse my Gavin of exaggerating a wee bit when he spins tales of his adventures, but when he claimed you were beautiful he was stating nothing more than the literal truth." She glanced at Gavin. "You must leave us alone for a few minutes," she told him, "to permit Miss Riggs and myself to become better acquainted."

Gavin nodded. "I shall wait in the hall," he told Justine. Looking at his mother, he said lightly, "I hope you won't burden Miss Riggs with any more of our family secrets. Only a few minutes ago I told her about Mrs. Mallory and her work."

"Have no fear," Mrs. Spencer told him. Their gazes met and held momentarily before Gavin turned and, with his white robes flowing behind him, left the room.

Mrs. Spencer nodded Justine to a chair beside her bed. "Do you find our Prospect Hall to your taste?" she asked. "It is rather a hodgepodge."

"Immensely," Justine said with enthusiasm. "I consider old houses so much more intriguing than modern ones and the Hall is such a marvelous collection of odd nooks and hidden crannies. I can imagine that a ghost would love to take up residence here."

"I suppose we have our ghosts," Mrs. Spencer said, seeming distracted for an instant. "But if ghosts there are, surely they must be only of the most amiable variety." She sighed. "I do worry so about Gavin," she said.

"I imagine any mother would worry if her son were constantly leaving home to sail to foreign shores."

"How very true. No one knows what diseases might be rampant in those foreign climes or what sort of exotic strangers a traveler might encounter or what temptations might lurk in those cities of the east. I do so worry about Gavin, he needs more than I can give him, he needs a steadying hand. When I married Gavin's father he was twenty-two and already my Gavin is ten years older than that. He should marry, and soon, before—" She paused. "Before the right season of his life, and there is a season for all things, has passed him by."

Justine, perplexed, wondering exactly what Mrs. Spencer was trying to tell her, said nothing.

"Do I embarrass you?" Mrs. Spencer asked. "I do have the reputation for speaking my mind," she went on without waiting for an answer. "To my way of thinking, a mother has the right to be concerned about her son, especially an only son, and Gavin and I have always been close, even more so since his father passed away. I *am* proud of Gavin, I hope you realize how very proud of him I am."

"You have every reason to be proud," Justine said, "having a son who is admired throughout England."

"Many mothers of gentlemen of achievement, and with all due modesty I include dear Gavin among that number, are apt to interfere in their sons' lives even after they marry. I want you to know, Miss Riggs, I am not that sort, not in the least."

Justine, puzzled by the twists and turnings of the conversation, said, "I had no reason to think you were, Mrs. Spencer."

"I suppose not, but one is constantly meeting those, and sadly they are women for the most part, women who spread tales that have not the slightest basis in fact. Tales of overbearing mothers, interfering mothers, mothers unwilling to recognize when the time has arrived to sever the silver cord. My wish is that everyone, not only you, my dear, becomes aware of my true feelings regarding my son."

How marvelous it would have been to have known a mother, Justine thought, no matter how overbearing or interfering, a mother who would love her and whom she would love despite any possible flaws. Those who had mothers should count their blessings.

"More than anything in the world," Mrs. Spencer went on, "I desire to see Gavin married. When he does marry, I will be more than willing to fade into the shadows of obscurity for good and all. Here at Prospect Hall, Gavin's wife will be the one to manage the household rather than myself and oversee the estate manager while Gavin is away from England on one of his expeditions."

Several moments passed before all the implications of what Mrs. Spencer had said became clear to Justine. "Do you mean," she asked, surprised, "that after Gavin is married you expect his wife to remain here at Prospect Hall rather than to be traveling with him?"

Now Mrs. Spencer appeared surprised in turn. "Traveling with him? Into the jungles of tropical Africa? To fight alongside the rebels in Greece? Oh my dear, Gavin would never allow any wife of his to take such risks."

Justine bit back her words of protest. She had supposed a wife would be allowed, if not expected or encouraged, to share her husband's life whether that meant taking risks or not. As she had been about so many things, she decided, she was probably wrong about this as well.

"My dear son," Mrs. Spencer said, "often travels to dangerous places where women are unwelcome, where they become more of a hindrance than a help. Not that any wife of Gavin's would be confined here at the Hall, we have a town house on Hanover Square and every autumn I visit my brother at Hallows near Leeds."

"Almost any woman should be more than satisfied with all of that," Justine said, chiding herself for expecting too much, for being unreasonable.

"Of course she would." Mrs. Spencer reached out, took Justine's hand and squeezed it affectionately. "I have so enjoyed our little chitchat," she said. "I *am* exhausted, the preparations for the ball, you know. Gavin so surprised me by insisting that we hold a ball, but after meeting you I can understand his reasons."

Flattered and yet made vaguely uneasy by Mrs. Spencer's laudatory words, she said, "The masquerade is proving a great success."

"Now," Mrs. Spencer said, "I must release you. I realize how anxious you must be to go to Gavin and to enjoy the dancing, I so liked to dance when I was young. My son must be equally eager for me to return you to him."

Justine rose and—murmuring her hope that Mrs. Spencer would soon be in the best of health—rejoined Gavin in the hallway. He glanced at her and then over her shoulder at the closed door to his mother's room, sighed and offered Justine his arm and escorted her down the stairs. "Though I love her very dearly," he said, "I find that sometimes my mother fails to understand. She treats me as though I were still a young boy."

In many ways, Justine told herself as they entered the ballroom, he seemed a boy—most men were—not only Gavin but Quentin as well. Which was part of their charm. As well as a constant source of exasperation. Quentin, for instance—Shaking her head, she paused in her thoughts, firmly reining them in. Whatever Quentin might be like, he no longer mattered to her.

She found Prudence barely able to suppress her curiosity. Once Gavin left them, bowing over Justine's hand, the older woman, all agog, said, "You were with Mr. Spencer for such a long time."

"Gavin showed me the Hall," Justine told her.

"And, after he introduced me to his mother, she and I had a most pleasant chat. She told me how much she worries about him."

"I understand she hopes he marries soon. Before he leaves England again."

"She did mention something of the sort," Justine admitted.

A short while later, alone with Gerard, Prudence said, "I have the most encouraging news to tell you. Mrs. Spencer had a long conversation with Justine on the subject of marriage, not marriage in general but her son's marriage in particular."

When Gerard met Ogden as they were helping themselves to generous portions of roast beef from the supper table, he said, "Just as I thought, young Spencer came home to England seeking a bride and has his eye on Justine Riggs. Only tonight, Prudence informs me, his mother met Justine and approved of her."

As Ogden reluctantly danced with Daphne, he said, between muttered apologies for his clumsiness, "Good as married according to Prudence, young Spencer and Justine, nothing left to do except set the date."

"Such wonderful news," Daphne told Quentin a few minutes later. "What a catch. He certainly cuts a dash."

"Who cuts a dash?" Quentin wanted to know. "And what is the wonderful news?"

"Gavin Spencer introduced Justine to his mother," Daphne explained, "and Mrs. Spencer simply adored her. Mr. Spencer subsequently asked Prudence for permission to propose marriage and, I do believe, he not only has done so but Justine has accepted him."

Quentin's eyebrows shot up; he glowered down at Daphne. Hastily excusing himself, he strode across the dance floor, his cape unfurled behind him, to where Justine was seated drinking punch as she talked to John Willoughby. "Come with me," Quentin told her.

When she stared defiantly up at him, he said again, louder this time, "Come with me."

"I say, Quentin," John began, "you really should be a bit more—"

Quentin motioned him away with a wave of his hand and John, after a glance at Justine who nodded, rose and walked sulkily off. Quentin remained standing, hands clenched at his sides, staring down at her.

"Why did you do it?" he demanded.

Why were the two of them always at daggers drawn, Justine wondered. "What on Earth are you talking about?" she asked.

"I have no need to explain, since you know perfectly well. You and Gavin Spencer. After an acquaintance of little more than a fortnight. Have you taken leave of your senses?"

Ah, she thought, he must have seen me alone with Gavin when he showed me around the Hall. Does that give him any right to consider me an abandoned woman? "What passed between Gavin and myself is none of your concern," she told him defiantly. "I did nothing improper."

"Foolhardy would be a better word. What do you know of the man after such a short acquaintance? Or do you believe one should act in blissful ignorance?"

"Gavin Spencer has always behaved like the gentleman he is while in my presence which is more, Lord Devon, than I can say for you."

"A gentleman? Does a gentleman practice deceit and deception?"

"What deception? There has been no deception."

"It so happens," Quentin said with a quickening note of triumph in his voice, "that those accounts of his expeditions which you find so enthralling were not written by Mr. Spencer but by a female scribbler named Alicia Mallory who, it seems, is living at Prospect Hall at this very moment."

Justine smiled. "I was aware of that," she told him. "Mr. Spencer has been quite above board with me; he himself informed me of the help Mrs. Mallory gives him in preparing his books for publication."

He blinked in surprise. "And that failed to change your obviously inflated opinion of him?"

"I thought it commendable of Gavin"—she put added emphasis on his given name—"to be so forthcoming."

Quentin shook his head. "You, Miss Riggs," he said, "are past praying for." He drew in a deep breath, seemingly in an attempt to regain his composure. "Under the circumstances," he told her, "all I can do is wish you my very best."

He bowed, turned abruptly on his heel and strode off leaving Justine staring after him in confused amaze-ment.

Fifteen

On the morning following the masquerade, Quentin Fletcher drove his curricle from the stable yard onto the avenue leading away from Kinsdale Manor. Oblivious to the heat of the summer sun and the dust raised by the wheels of his carriage, he stared straight ahead as he tried to bring order to the jumble of his roiling emotions.

He was returning to town by driving through Tyburn to the London road as, he ruefully reminded himself, he should have done long before this. He had learned many years before, that once the tide turns, whether at the gaming tables or in the affairs of men, only a King Canute or a someone equally foolish or a believer in miracles continues to stand his ground.

He was well rid of her.

She was a perverse creature, she was stubborn to the point of being intractable, she was willful, she demanded a greater commitment than any reasonable gentleman could be expected to give, she was terribly naive, she lacked a dowry of any sort, she was practically devoid of the customary feminine talents (unless singing sea chanties qualified), she refused to be amiable (at least to him), she insisted on challenging a man rather than graciously acceding to his simplest wishes, she was—

Quentin shook his head. He could go on listing her failings, he could go on almost indefinitely, but why should he bother? His case was proved, there was no room for any debate.

And now she had shown how fickle she was. Only a few days before, she had given every evidence of having a tenderness for him—with a pang of loss he relived that moment when she was in his arms beneath the swaying branches of the weeping willow—and yet last night she had accepted an offer of marriage from Gavin Spencer, a mere chance acquaintance, a pig in a poke, an adventurer she had known for little more than a sennight.

It occurred to him that it might appear to a casual, neutral observer, to Rodgers for example, that he was being a tad inconsistent. True enough, he *had* considered encouraging a liaison between Spencer and Justine, he freely admitted having entertained such a notion at one time. But that was before he had chanced on Mrs. Mallory in the west wing, Spencer's secret writer in residence. Men who practiced deceit rarely stopped with one deception, trickery became a habit with them. Who could tell what other secrets Prospect Hall concealed?

But what of yourself? he demanded in an attempt to do justice to Spencer for he had always been, Quentin assured himself, a fair-minded man. *What do you call your so-called retreat on Whitechapel Road if not a deception? Have you stopped with one such ruse or are there others? To take it a step further, have you ever thought that perhaps you, Quentin Fletcher, practice deception not only on others but on yourself as well?*

What utter nonsense! Whitechapel Road can hardly be compared to Mrs. Mallory. I can say this with certainty because, unlike many others, I have a clear and complete understanding of the workings of my own mind. And of my heart as well. And since I am fully cognizant of what is in my long-term best interest, I intend to act accordingly.

No one can claim my departing the Manor this morning is the act of a spurned and therefore a defeated man. Or even of a man in temporary retreat who fully intends to marshal his forces for a triumphant return to the scene of his setback. Setback? Ha! Even now, all I would have to do to have her come to me is snap my fingers. That I choose not to snap them is my decision, arrived at after long and careful consideration.

When I refused to meet her demands—to be fair to her, and I have always been fair in all my dealings with women as well as men, I might better term them her expectations rather than her demands since she was clever enough never to state them outright—and declined to offer her marriage, what did she do? Just as a ocean voyager who, after watching the ship bearing her hopes for the future slowly sink beneath the waves, grasps at any flotsam, at any stray driftage, she in her desperation immediately reached out and took hold of Mr. Gavin Spencer.

And welcome to him, I say. I shall fare very well without Justine Riggs.

There are, after all, many other desirable young women in this world, women who combine beauty, amiability and talent. Phillippa, to name only one, if a man can learn to abide her inane chatter; and Marianne, even though her giggle quickly begins to grate on one's nerves; and Clothilde, whose shameless flirtatiousness will certainly cease when she marries (or will it become even more flagrant?); and Claire, whose generous dowry will, I suppose, make it possible for any sensible and far-seeing man such as myself to overlook her unbounded affection for her, at last count, twenty-eight house cats.

A man had to try to ignore the minor faults of women, he told himself, for what man was perfect? Each had his faults, both great and small, in fact he must have them himself although he was unable to enumerate any at the moment.

Reaching the top of a low hill, Quentin reined in his horse to gaze down at the village of Tyburn and, a mile farther on, the curling ribbon of the road to London. He had promised himself he would not look back, either figuratively or literally, but now he broke that promise by turning in his seat for a last glimpse of Kinsdale Manor.

To Quentin, the Manor, with its overgrown topiary garden, its brick chimneys leaning at rakish angles and the rampant growth of ivy that threatened to blind the house by covering each and every one of its windows, seemed as dreary and forlorn as his own mood.

He was about to turn away and drive down the hill into Tyburn when he saw a lone horseman approaching the country house along a lane beyond the Manor. Gavin Spencer. Whatever his faults, Quentin conceded, the man did know how to sit a horse. And how in character for Spencer to waste so little time in calling on his bride-to-be. In all likelihood the marriage would follow within the month and Mr. and Mrs. Spencer would depart from England for parts unknown before the leaves turned.

While he, Quentin, would be left with Whitechapel Road and whatever consolation he might obtain there. Despite his vow not to dwell on the past, he wondered whether Spencer might very well be getting the better of the bargain. Acknowledging with a sigh his feeling of incompleteness, Quentin flipped the ribbons and started down the hill to Tyburn, aware that in some way he had left a vital part of himself behind at Kinsdale Manor with Justine Riggs . . .

At the Manor, Bessie, Daphne's abigail, was the first to note Gavin Spencer's approach. "Well, fancy that," she said with evident admiration. "He looks like the lord of the Earth."

When Daphne came to stand beside her maid at the bedchamber window, she could only agree that Gavin Spencer cut a dashing figure. Surpassingly fashionable in a vivid blue waistcoat and a gold cravat, to her he seemed to be the wild Viking warrior of her imaginings tamed and transformed into an urbane English gentleman.

His elegant dress combined with his sober demeanor told her that his was to be more than a social call. After giving instructions to Bessie and repeating them twice, she summoned Ogden and Gerard to the drawing room and, meeting them there, told the two men what she had seen and what she suspected.

"A proposal of marriage from Spencer?" an agape Ogden repeated. "So soon?"

"I devoutly hope so," Daphne said.

"Gavin Spencer is a man accustomed to seizing the moment," Gerard reminded Ogden, "a man who strikes while the iron is hot."

There was a tapping at the door and Bessie entered to whisper a few words in Daphne's ear.

"You see," she cried as soon as her maid left the room, her voice raised in triumph, "I was quite correct. Mr. Spencer has asked to pay his respects to Prudence and at this moment is being shown to her sitting room."

Gerard nodded. "To win her permission to speak to Justine. There can be no other logical explanation."

"Capital, capital." Ogden rubbed his hands together. "Shall we toast the success of our modest enterprise? We three, with the help of Prudence, of course, are responsible for this happy turn of events."

"We should not assume success quite yet," Daphne warned him, "you forget that Justine must first accept Mr. Spencer's suit. The final nail still remains to be hammered into place. No chain can be stronger than its weakest link."

"Is there any doubt what her answer will be?" Gerard asked. "We decided, after considerable investigation, that he was the ideal candidate for her hand and my respect for the man grows with each passing day. Besides, Justine has no other prospects."

Ogden started to speak, stopped, rumbled deep in his throat. "It has never been my pleasure," he said at last, "to encounter a more perverse young lady than

Miss Justine Riggs. What we all agree she *should* do may have no bearing whatsoever on what she *will* do."

"And so," Daphne said, "it behooves us to guide her to the proper decision. While Mr. Spencer is closeted with Prudence, let all three of us encourage her to arrive at the only reasonable response. Do you agree?"

Both men nodded.

"Since Prudence will give her permission without giving the matter much thought," Daphne said "we have precious little time and so we must not dally. Justine is, I believe, in the conservatory."

At that very moment Justine, her white muslin morning dress clinging to her body in the hot moist air, was gazing in puzzled concern into a birdcage hanging at one end of the conservatory, a large room containing Gerard's collection of vines and broadleafed tropical plants, their tendrils and branches reaching up toward a skylight in the roof. Inside the silver cage, a canary sat silent and unmoving on his perch. Although Justine had visited the conservatory several times since coming to the Manor, she had never heard the bird sing.

Her heart going out to what she saw as the bird's unhappiness, on impulse she unlatched the cage door, swung it open and stepped back. The canary fluttered to the opening where it hesitated, darting its head uncertainly to the right and the left before returning to its accustomed place on the perch.

Hearing a sound behind her, Justine turned to find Daphne, Ogden and Gerard entering the conservatory. As soon as they were all seated, Justine on an iron bench, the others on chairs, Daphne said with a note of urgency, "Mr. Spencer is at this very moment conversing with Prudence and the subject of that conversation is, we are certain, none other than yourself."

Justine gasped. Although she had been half expecting something of the sort, she was still surprised that Gavin had wasted so little time in approaching Prudence. Since she had believed she would have time to give his proposal the most careful consideration—she was almost certain that was what brought him here—she now felt a sense of being unduly and unfairly hurried.

Without preamble, Daphne said, "I need not remind you it is the duty of a young lady to wed."

Gerard nodded. "Not only is it her duty but in all likelihood marriage will be the source of her greatest happiness. Of all the years of my life, and there have been more than three score, the happiest year by far, and unfortunately there was only one, was when I experienced the comfort and bliss of a congenial marriage to an angelic young lady."

Ogden frowned, blinked, clasped his hands and then said, "I find myself unable to imagine a more appropriate suitor than Mr. Gavin Spencer. He is, in the opinion of all who know him, as well as to my way of thinking, a true paragon."

Justine, feeling herself beset from all sides, could only nod her head.

"My greatest regret," Daphne said with a sigh, "is that I never married. A woman may write novels that are admired by thousands of readers but, if she never marries, she must be counted a failure; a woman may devote her life to charitable societies and the performance of good works but, if she never marries, the world can only offer her the most grudging praise; a woman may be witty and charming and amiable for all of her days but, if she never marries, she has wasted her talents on barren soil."

"Surely," Justine objected, "you overstate the perils of spinsterhood. There must be something to be said for being beholden only to yourself."

"Overstate? I believe I understate," Daphne told her. "Unless she is most fortunate, unless she has kind friends and generous relatives, a spinster is doomed to a life of loneliness and, more often than not, poverty."

"I have always deeply regretted," Gerard said, "and especially as the years have ever more rapidly slipped away, that I never had any children. How else is it possible for a man or a woman to leave a lasting imprint on the future than through marrying and raising a family?"

"And in Mr. Gavin Spencer," Ogden put in with an emphatic nod, "we have a gentleman admired by all, the cynosure of every eye whether male or female, a man most women would agree to marry in a trice if only fortunate enough to be given the opportunity."

That, Justine admitted to herself, was undoubtedly true.

"And you must never forget," Daphne said, "that when a woman marries she not only benefits herself but her family as well. Or, when there is no immediate family, as is, alas, your situation, she benefits those who have been her friends and benefactors. Only through marriage is a young lady able to cease being a burden on those who have lavished their love and care upon her."

216

Justine nodded her agreement since, more than any other argument she had heard, this one struck home. She realized she was under an enormous obligation to Prudence Baldwin and that only through an advantageous marriage could she ever hope to repay that debt.

Hearing Daphne draw in a quick breath, she followed her gaze to the doorway.

Gavin Spencer, smiling, bowed to them all.

"We really must excuse ourselves," Daphne told him with a flutter of her hand. Murmuring apologies and talking vaguely of going for a ramble in the park, she hurried Ogden and Gerard from the conservatory.

As Justine watched him with a feeling of unease, Gavin walked slowly to her and raised her hand to his lips. If he was about to propose marriage, and she strongly suspected he was, what should her reply be? she wondered. There was only one reasonable answer she could give him and yet, unhappily aware she was being hastened toward matrimony by her friends, she felt an urge to be unreasonable.

Gavin was about to sit on the bench beside her when he noticed the open door of the canary cage. Stepping away from her with a murmured apology, he latched the door shut. "The bird is so accustomed to being fed and cared for by humans," he said, "she could never survive outside her cage."

Although she had to agree with him, Justine asked herself if the canary, so unhappy in its cage, might not prefer a few days of freedom to a life of imprisonment.

Gavin, returning to sit at her side, remarked briefly on the sultry weather and the success of the masquerade ball, carefully observing her response, much as a military commander might reconnoiter an enemy position before launching his attack. Finally taking her hand in his, he said, "As you are probably aware, Justine, I come to you after a most cordial interview with Mrs. Baldwin. Your guardian gave me nothing but encouragement."

He paused as though expecting Justine to comment but when she said nothing he plunged resolutely on. "I have grown exceedingly fond of you in a very brief time, my dear Justine," he said, "and have come to admire not only your beauty but your independence of spirit as well. For many years I have been aware of the disadvantages of bachelorhood, have recognized the rewards of journeying through life with an amiable companion such as yourself. I could, I suppose, deliver a lengthy speech praising you and extolling the merits of marriage but I happen to be a man who believes in being direct." Raising her hand to his lips, he said, "Will you, Justine, do me the honor of becoming my wife?"

Drawing her hand away, Justine started to speak only to stop and look away from him, uncharacteristically at a loss for words.

Gavin broke the silence. "I realize," he said, "I may be behaving rashly by approaching you after such a brief acquaintance but at the ball last night you gave me every reason to hope, nay, to expect, you would give me a favorable reply."

Justine rose and walked to the birdcage where she stared, unseeing, at the songless canary. Had she somehow encouraged Gavin by her behavior at the ball? she asked herself, striving to remember all that had occurred there. With a shock, she realized that when she recalled the masquerade, most of the evening was a pleasant blur, the elegant dancers, Gavin's daring leap from balcony to balcony and her meeting with Mrs. Spencer in Gavin's mother's chambers. On the other hand, the few minutes she had spent in a bitter dispute with Quentin remained crystal-clear in her mind.

Quentin was, no matter how often she might try to reject the notion or how vehemently she might deny the fact, the man she loved now and would love forever. Without Quentin, her future was ashes. To accept Gavin's proposal would be unfair not only to herself but to Gavin as well.

Turning to him, she said, "You do me great honor, but I must decline, not because I lack respect for you, or fault you in any way, but because I lack feelings of tenderness for you."

"If you were to take a few days to give the matter more thought—"

Justine immediately shook her head. She started to reach out to touch his sleeve but drew her hand away. "No," she said, "time will only confirm my feelings."

"I could not fail to notice," he said with a tinge of bitterness, "that when I touch you, you instinctively move away and when I take your hand you withdraw it as soon as you possibly can. It occurs to me that you, like many young women, are uncomfortable when confronted with the less spiritual aspects of marriage, with what might be viewed as the satisfaction of male lusts rather than the more affectionate expressions of love."

Justine stared at him in confusion. She might be

curious as well as the least bit apprehensive about what awaited her in the marriage bed but she failed to find the idea of the union of a man and a woman who loved one another in any way repugnant.

"If you are uncomfortable," Gavin went on, obviously choosing his words with great care, "I can assure you that in my case any fears you may have in that regard are completely groundless. The consuming passions of my life happen to be exploration and discovery, all of my energies are consumed in my work and my other interests. Therefore you, Justine, although you would be my wife and my companion, would be spared the forced intimacy you may fear. There are those who, if they knew the truth about me, would look askance, nay, they would condemn me out of hand, but this is the way God made me and this is the way, for better or worse, I am."

Was he trying to assuage what he suspected to be her fears or was he revealing his true nature? she wondered. Since Gavin had never dissembled even when it was in his best interests to do so, she supposed he was being truthful now. Although not quite certain what his words implied—in fact she was made vaguely uncomfortable by them—she did know that this final appeal of his had missed its mark.

"Mr. Spencer," she said softly, intending to spare hurting him if at all possible, "my answer must be, will always be, the same, and any further discussion will fail to alter that answer and can only result in pain for both of us."

He sighed and bowed in acknowledgement and acceptance. "I wish—" he began but seemed to think better of making any further protest and turned away from Justine and walked stiffly from the conservatory . . .

Lord Alton watched Gavin Spencer leave the Manor, deducing from Spencer's scowl of chagrin and disappointment that his mission had been unsuccessful. How intriguing, he told himself, especially since the night before, he had seen Quentin Fletcher in a high dudgeon after speaking with Justine and earlier this morning he had observed a disgruntled Quentin Fletcher depart, bag and baggage.

Removing a jeweled snuffbox from the pocket of his waistcoat, Lord Alton took a pinch of snuff and inserted it in his right nostril. Taking another pinch, he inserted it in his left nostril. With his mouth closed, he breathed in deeply. After sneezing lustily, he dabbed the spittle from his face with a lace handkerchief.

Spencer was gone, Fletcher was gone. Realizing that this left him in sole possession of the field, Lord Alton smiled. Quite unexpectedly, he found himself without competition. Not that he expected to accomplish his goal through honorable means, for Lord Alton had never considered himself to be an honorable man. One of his great strengths, in his opinion, was that he had never been troubled by a conscience; another was his willingness to go to any lengths to have his way; still another was his lack of scruples.

His goal was simple: he wanted Justine Riggs and, with Fletcher and Spencer both gone, his time had come. He knew he must act swiftly since in the next day or two the house party guests at the Manor would be on their way back to London. The vague outlines of a scheme to accomplish his ends was already taking shape in his mind.

A bit more thought followed by careful preparation and then Justine, willingly or not, would be his.

Sixteen

Lord Alton sat in the half-light of his chambers at Kinsdale Manor with the drapes drawn, his chin resting on his steepled hands. For as long as he could remember, he had shunned the daylight, finding that darkness gave him an almost sensual pleasure. When in London he often prowled the echoing streets late at night, seeking the unexpected encounter or the bizarre entertainment, eager to sample the secret, erotic delights offered by the dark underside of the city.

Until this morning he had been impatient to return to town but now, with the sudden and unexpected departure of Lord Devon followed by the rebuff obviously suffered by Gavin Spencer, his mood had abruptly changed from one of weary sufferance to one of keen anticipation. His blood raced with the excitement of the hunt, the expectation of first outfoxing and then ensnaring his prey, of making her his to do with as he pleased.

Closing his eyes, he pictured her as he had seen her the night before at the masquerade, her black hair short and curled, the exquisite curves of her body invitingly revealed by the tight-fitting leggings and the belted tunic of her Robin Hood costume, her flashing dark eyes and slightly parted lips hinting of a long suppressed passion seething just beneath the placid surface of her facade of virginal innocence.

Justine Riggs was naive while at the same time she was a woman of daring, a tantalizing and dangerous combination. Tantalizing to him; dangerous for her. Lord Alton had first realized how bold she was when he became aware of her tryst with Devon beneath the weeping willow. Recognizing the two horses beside the stream, he knew at once that the two of them had ridden to the meadow to be alone together. Pretending to see nothing, he had ridden on, but now he intended to make good use of his knowledge.

Smiling to himself, he imagined her as his prisoner. Helpless. Completely in his power. His to do with as he wished. He had pictured her this way many times during the last few weeks, seeing her with her hands tied behind her, an imploring look on her lovely face as she pleaded with him. God, how this vision of her helplessness excited him.

He imagined reaching to her and unbuttoning her tunic to reveal the rise of her breasts and the shadowed valley between them. She cringed away from him, obviously afraid, nay, terrorized, and yet when he stroked the bare flesh of her shoulder he saw something besides fear in her eyes, he recognized the vivid spark of hidden desire.

Enough, he told himself, opening his eyes and shaking his head. He was not a man who was satisfied by mere imaginings. He wanted Justine Riggs and he would have her. This very day.

Lord Alton rose and walked to the window where he thrust aside the draperies, squinting in the sudden glare of the noonday sun. Crossing the room to the desk, he stood rummaging through a thick and disordered pile of papers until he unearthed the two-month-old letter from Devon.

Although politely phrased, the brief note was a dunning demand for monies owed by Lord Alton in the sum of three hundred and fifty guineas. The gambling debt, only one of many, was so ancient that Alton could no longer recall the occasion of his loss. He chortled with malicious glee. How fortunate, he told himself, that his procrastination in satisfying the debt— he would, of course, since he was a gentleman, deliver the paltry sum but only when it pleased him to do so— had resulted in his friend Devon taking pen in hand to request payment.

Sitting at the desk, Alton placed Devon's letter to one side before opening a drawer and removing several blank sheets of paper. Using a quill, he penned a brief note, scowling as he read and then reread it. Following prolonged thought, he proceeded to cross out words and add others until he was moderately pleased with the result:

My dear Justine,
>I acted the fool. Will you ever
>forgive me?
>I must see you. Alone. Tonight
>at ten beneath the willow.
>Tell no one.

Alton

After once more reading what he had written, he was still not satisfied. Should he address her as "My dear Justine"? Perhaps simply "Dearest" without her name. No, her name must appear on the note but he settled on "My dearest Justine" as sounding appropriately intimate. The signature, "Alton," seemed wrong; he should use his given name, Vail, or just the initial, V. Yes, V struck the right note. Should he warn her his life would not be worth living if she failed to come to him? Or hint he was in deadly danger? No, those touches would be much too melodramatic.

He rewrote the message with the changes. The result was imperfect, he admitted, but it was the best he could do and would be good enough. Taking still another sheet of paper, he wrote another note, using the same wording except for one small but vital alteration. This note he wrote several times, imitating Devon's flowing handwriting.

When he was finally satisfied, Alton folded and sealed both of the messages. As soon as the wax had hardened, he broke one of the seals and unfolded the letter, wrinkling it slightly. He placed three guineas in a neat pile on the desk beside the two letters, frowned and added two more.

His preparations were complete. "Now let the hunt begin," he murmured to himself . . .

Later that afternoon, Justine was strolling along a path in one of the Manor's neglected gardens when she heard Daphne calling her name. Turning, she waited until the other woman hurried to join her.

"Have you heard the news?" Daphne asked, evidently hoping she had not. "The news concerning Lord Devon?"

"Oh, yes." Justine, having been told of Quentin's departure several hours before, was able to keep any hint of her disappointment from her voice. "He left for town this morning. Everyone seemed surprised he had stayed at the Manor as long as he did."

Daphne shook her head. "No, no, not that news. Only seconds ago I learned that after leaving the Manor with the announced intention of driving to London, Lord Devon actually drove no further than Tyburn. At this very moment he is lodging at the Unicorn Inn in the village." She raised her eyebrows. "Have you ever heard of such strange behavior, making everyone believe he was on his way to town and then going only a few miles? We all wonder what his motives might be."

"Are you certain he went only as far as Tyburn?" Justine asked. Was it possible Quentin changed his mind about going to London because of her?

Daphne raised both hands as though to ask how certain she was expected to be. "If you mean, did I see Lord Devon in Tyburn myself, no, I did not, but one of the Kinsdale stableboys not only saw him arrive at the inn but was told by the hostler that he had engaged a room there. A most peculiar business all around."

What could Quentin be about? Justine had no ready answer and was still pondering his possible reasons for changing his mind when, on leaving the drawing room after taking tea later in the afternoon, she heard her name called and saw Hodgkins approaching carrying his silver tray.

Hodgkins, she noticed, was no longer the slouching servant she had encountered when she arrived at the Manor. Some days before she had glimpsed him walking with a wine glass on his head as Rodgers stood nearby nodding his approval. Now, erect and well-groomed, he seemed every inch a butler.

"A letter for you, miss," Hodgkins explained when she gave him a puzzled look.

Taking the letter from his tray, she turned away from the butler before tearing open the seal. "My dearest Justine," she read, "I acted the fool. Will you ever forgive me? I must see you. Alone. Tonight at ten beneath the willow. Tell no one." The message was signed, "Q."

Her breath caught. Although she had never seen his handwriting, she knew the message must be from Quentin for only he knew about their encounter beneath the willow. So he *had* stayed in Tyburn because of her. Was he in trouble of some kind? In danger? Did he need her help?

Turning to question Hodgkins, she found him lingering a few paces away running his white-gloved forefinger along the ridge at the top of a door lintel.

"This letter," she said, sensing Hodgkins had tarried because he expected her to question him. "Do you know who brought the letter here?"

"A lad from Tyburn," he told her. "Said a gentleman at the inn gave him a shilling to deliver it."

She nodded and, thanking him, turned away.

Her first impulse was to go to the willow at ten, to go to Quentin. Why, though, did he want her to meet him not only in secret but in the dark of the night? There was a wrongness about his request that troubled her since he was well aware that if she were discovered with him, their being together would make a spicy broth of scandal certain to be savored by the gossips of the *ton*.

228

On the other hand, she longed to see him again, to have his comforting arms enfold her, to feel his lips warm on hers. She tingled at the thought. But how frightfully foolish it would be to meet Quentin knowing that seeing him now would only make their parting, when it came as come it inevitably must, unendurably painful.

She would not go.

Her decision made, she sat through a lengthy dinner even though her appetite had deserted her. After the final course, Gerard proposed an evening of whist, a suggestion applauded by his guests. When they prepared to play, however, Gerard made an annoying discovery.

"Unfortunately," he announced to one and all, "we find ourselves with thirteen players."

Without conscious thought, Justine said, "I feel slightly out of sorts tonight so I believe I should go to bed early rather than play."

"You do look feverish," Prudence concurred, "and I noticed you ate hardly anything at all at dinner. Not enough to keep a bird alive."

Excusing herself, Justine hurried up the stairs. As soon as she closed the door of her bedchamber behind her, she changed into her Robin Hood costume. There was no doubt in her mind that being the thirteenth player at whist had been an omen telling her to do as Quentin requested.

She crept down the rear stairs and, she was almost certain, slipped from the house without being seen. Although the first stars were beginning to appear in the clear sky, the last rose-tinted light of the dying day lingered in the west. After hurrying through the kitchen garden, she turned away from the Manor, deciding to walk the mile or more to the willow, realizing that asking for a horse from the stable would only call attention to herself.

As she walked along the lane in the deepening dusk, she listened to the sounds of the night, the evening songs of the birds, the croaking of frogs from a nearby pond and the barking of dogs in the Manor kennel. Hearing a rumbling ahead of her, she peered into the gloom and saw the outline of an approaching wagon. Rather than risk being seen and perhaps recognized, she hastily left the lane, climbed into and out of a ditch, and hid behind a hedge, anxiously watching through the branches as the wagon—returning from the fields, and carrying two farm laborers, both hunched on the raised seat—drove past her.

Detesting the necessity to hide, ashamed to be skulking about in the dark like a footpad, Justine debated whether she should return to the Manor. No, she had made up her mind, she would go to Quentin. He was depending on her, he would never forgive her if she failed him, she would never forgive herself.

She returned to the lane and walked on, finally seeing the dark silhouette of the willow looming against the faint glow on the horizon. Leaving the lane, she crossed the meadow, cautiously approaching the tree, all the while listening for the sound of Quentin's tethered horse but hearing nothing except the murmur of the stream.

When her groping hands touched the trailing branches of the willow, she hesitated, warning herself that this was her last chance to turn back. What, she wondered, would happen when, in a few minutes, she would be with Quentin? Recalling the other time they had met here, she sighed with pleasure at the memory of his embrace. The die, she realized, had been cast then and so, come what may, it was already too late for her to change her mind. Tingling with a fear laced with anticipation, she used both hands to spread aside the hanging fronds and stepped into the deeper darkness beneath the canopy of the tree.

"Quentin?" she called softly.

There was no answer.

"Quentin?" she called again, louder than before.

A man's form separated itself from the enshrouding shadows and walked slowly toward her. Quentin? Hands gripped her arms, pulling her forward and, for an instant, she leaned to him, ready to surrender herself to his embrace, but almost at once she felt an urgent sense of wrongness and instinctively drew back.

"Quentin?" Now her voice was sharp and wary.

"No, not Quentin, this is Alton."

Dumbfounded and startled, she gasped. "Let me go," she demanded. After the briefest hesitation, he released her and she stepped away from him. "Where is Quentin?" she wanted to know.

"To the best of my knowledge," Lord Alton said in his nasal drawl, "our good friend Quentin is in London. At least I was told he was bound for town when he left the Manor this morning."

She fought back panic. Shaking her head, not wanting to believe him, she said, "The stableboy saw him at the inn in Tyburn."

"I paid the boy to bring that bit of false information to the Manor."

"His letter, Quentin's letter—"

Justine's breath caught in her throat as she realized the truth. Lord Alton had written the letter and signed it with Quentin's initial. But how had he known about the willow? Of course, Alton must have seen her with Quentin on the day he rode past the meadow.

She turned to flee.

"Wait." Alton's voice rang as cold and sharp as a steel blade. "Before you try to run, hear me out. You may change your mind about leaving."

While she hesitated, he said, "I can easily overtake you if you dash off but I dislike violence, especially when it's really so unnecessary."

Justine shivered. What did he want with her? Could he actually be threatening to force her? She had never liked Alton, had from the first felt an unease in his presence and had distrusted him ever since and now her worst fears were being borne out. Was he merely trying to frighten her? Would he dare try to do more?

"You must concede, my dear," he told her, "that in the eyes of the world you came here to meet me, absolutely alone and in the dark of night."

"You tricked me into coming."

"Tricked you? How did I trick you?" From the tone of his voice, she could sense his self-satisfied smile. "I gave a boy in Tyburn a message to deliver to the Manor, a message asking you to meet me here. You came freely, even eagerly."

"You made me think the letter came from Lord Devon." Her distaste for him tinged her voice with acid.

"If you decide to behave in an unreasonable manner," he said, "the boy will swear that I, not Lord Devon, gave him a shilling to deliver the message to you at the Manor, which will be no more than the truth. Not only will the boy so testify, a letter will be discovered in your chambers asking you to meet me here, a letter in my handwriting and signed by myself, not by Devon. Your denials will be seen as nothing more than the desperate pleadings of a guilty young woman."

Justine backed away from him, shaking her head.

He said, "I have little liking for rustic surroundings such as these. Perhaps if we could—"

Justine spun around and ran. Alton sprang after her, his hand grasping her arm and swinging her toward him. She clawed at him, her nails raking the side of his face, and she heard his sharp intake of breath. Twisting out of his grasp, she ran blindly, ran as hard as she could only to trip and sprawl face down on the ground.

She turned on her side and looked up. Though she couldn't see Alton in the darkness, she heard his footsteps coming nearer and nearer, then stopping and retreating. Peering around her, she saw what appeared to be a column darker than the surrounding gloom. The trunk of the willow. Cautiously, her body aching from her fall, she crawled to the tree and crouched behind it, afraid that if she ran, Alton would hear her steps and find her.

She thought she heard the rustle of fronds. Holding her breath, she listened but the sound wasn't repeated. Did Alton think she had left the shelter of the tree or was he patiently poised only a few feet away listening for some sound that would reveal her hiding place? Vainly trying to quell the pounding of her heart, she waited breathlessly, hoping against hope he would decide she had escaped into the meadow.

Each passing minute buoyed her hopes, easing the cold grip of fear. He had given up, she told herself, he had left. But she heard no sound of retreating hoofbeats, only the rustle of the night breeze in the branches around her and the whisper of the nearby brook.

A light appeared and disappeared. She blinked. Had she really seen a light? Yes, there it was again, the bobbing of a light seeming to flash on and off through the screen of the willow branches. Alton had left only to return with a lanthorn. When she saw him part the branches, she drew back behind the tree and, as he paced to and fro, she frantically tried to keep in the shadow of the willow's trunk.

The light was lowered and stopped moving as though he had placed the lanthorn on the ground. Alton's grotesque shadow appeared on the pale fronds behind her. Her breath caught. Suddenly Alton loomed over her, smiling in triumph. She whirled away from him but he was on her at once, bearing her to the ground, tearing at her clothes.

She screamed.

"Enough!"

Alton froze. She looked past him at the figure of a man, his face in the shadows. Who was he?

"On your feet." The newcomer's long-barreled pistol pointed menacingly at Alton.

Alton rolled away from her and slowly pushed himself up.

"Are you all right?" When the armed man turned slightly to look down at her, the light struck one side of his face.

Only then did she recognize him. Rodgers! Justine nodded uncertainly at him. Rising, she edged away from Alton.

"Have you gone mad?" Alton asked, advancing slowly on Rodgers.

"Take one more step," Rodgers warned, the pistol steady in his hand, "and I fire." His voice was calm but deadly.

Alton stopped.

"Listen to me," Rodgers told him, "and listen well as though your life depended on it because it does. If you come near Miss Riggs ever again I shall seek you out and I shall kill you. In cold blood, without warning, without preamble and without a sporting chance of any sort. Being only a humble servant, my lord, I will have no compunction whatsoever in killing you, no need to follow a gentleman's code of honor." He paused. "Do you understand?"

For several minutes, Lord Alton said nothing. Finally he nodded. "I understand," he muttered.

"Capital." Rodgers motioned with his pistol. "You will now depart, my lord," he said, "and that will be the end of this little misunderstanding. Unless—" He allowed the threat to remain unfinished.

Alton turned on his heel and pushed through the willow fronds. A few minutes later Justine heard the sound of hoofbeats fading into the distance.

Now, with the danger past, tears stung her eyes and she began to shiver uncontrollably. She hugged herself. Rodgers came to her and put a comforting, fatherly arm around her shoulders and she leaned against him while she drew in ragged breaths.

After long moments she recovered enough to step

away from him and dab at her tears. "How can I ever thank you for what you did?" she asked.

Rodgers smiled. "Thank me? I should be the one to thank you. All my rather drab life I've dreamed of heroically rescuing a young lady in distress and now you've given me the opportunity."

"Would you really have shot Lord Alton?"

"Oh, yes, certainly. To shoot a lord, particularly this lord, would have given me great satisfaction. Robin Hood"—he nodded at her Sherwood Forest garb— "found that a bow and arrow was a wonderful leveler of the classes. A pistol is even better."

"Did you see me leave the Manor tonight?" she asked. "And follow me here?"

Shaking his head, Rodgers said, "Not at all. The stableboy Alton hired happened to be the red-haired boy you told me was having a problem with a horse. I befriended him, suggested keeping an animal in the horse's stall, and today the lad, suspecting skulduggery of some sort, told me what he knew and so I followed Alton. The bastard." Rodgers inclined his head. "Pray pardon my crude language."

"Pardon you? Why should I have to pardon you when your word describes him perfectly?"

"Just so. Lord Alton, I suspect, will have left the Manor before morning. And you will have nothing to fear from him later when you return to London."

"London?" She drew a deep, shuddering breath. "No, Rodgers, I've had quite enough of the so-called gentlemen of the *ton*. I intend to make my home in Gravesend, not in London."

Seventeen

Rodgers, his arms folded, gazed across White-chapel Road at the Lord Devon's narrow, three-storied house. So this was Devon's famous—or perhaps infamous would be the better word—retreat from the world—this modest, aging structure built of red bricks placed in uneven rows as though by a slightly besotted bricklayer.

He crossed the cobbled street, climbed the narrow steps to the small porch, raised the brass knocker and rapped three times. There was no sound from inside the house. After patiently waiting for several minutes, Rodgers knocked again, louder and more insistently. The faint tapping of footsteps came from inside, he heard the rasp of a bolt being drawn and the door was flung open.

Rodgers, who prided himself on being remarkably imperturbable, drew back in surprise. Whoever he had expected to answer his knock—an aged manservant in old-fashioned livery, perhaps—he was not prepared to be greeted at the door by Lord Devon himself. Not only Lord Devon but a Lord Devon—a gentleman usually garbed in the height of fashion, sans waistcoat and sans cravat—a Lord Devon who wore trousers marred by inelegant wrinkles and creases.

Despite his discomfiture, Rodgers managed a deferential bow.

"Do you bring a message?" Quentin asked eagerly.

Rodgers shook his head.

"Is this more in the nature of a call on a matter of business?" Quentin asked him.

"You might term it that," Rodgers said.

Quentin raised his eyebrows but said nothing. With a weary shrug of his shoulders, he stood aside. When Rodgers hesitated, Devon said, "Come in, Rodgers, and when you do, pray stop staring at me as though I had broken some code of sartorial honor. You will allow me to dress as I see fit in the privacy of my own rooms, will you not?"

"Of course, my lord," Rodgers said, stepping into the entry.

As Quentin led him along the hall, Rodgers took care not to look about him, not wanting to appear overly inquisitive. It was impossible, however, not to notice the sparse and inelegant furnishings both in the hallway and in the interiors of whatever rooms he was able to glimpse from the corners of his eyes.

"My living quarters are on the ground floor," Quentin told him, "the upper rooms are used only for storage." He opened a door toward the rear of the house. "This is where I spend most of my time when I come here to Whitechapel Road."

Rodgers had been surprised that Quentin had taken it upon himself to answer the front door; he was even more surprised at what he now saw. The large chamber, well lighted by hanging oil lamps, rose two stories high with windows only on the back wall and those at least fifteen feet above the floor. The walls themselves were completely devoid of decoration.

The room was furnished with four long wooden tables, each containing an assortment of devices that Rodgers could not identify—iron cylinders girded by wires, black oblongs of metal protruding from large glass containers with wires looping away to black boxes, two silver balls, both larger than a man's head, mounted on the top of two long wooden poles rising almost to the ceiling, and wires, wires everywhere, strung endlessly back and forth between posts. At one side of the room was a desk cluttered with papers, several chairs and a cot covered by a blanket.

"A laboratory?" Rodgers ventured.

"Quite right." Quentin threw his hand aloft in a sweeping gesture taking in the room and its equipment. "I have always had an abiding interest," he said, "in electricity, its properties and its possible uses. Hence, this laboratory."

Rodgers shook his head. "I admit to being completely flabbergasted."

"During the last few years," Quentin said as he led Rodgers across the room, "my efforts have turned to the problem of sending messages across great distances by means of an instrument known as a telegraph."

"And that accounts for these wires?"

"Precisely. We have known for years that electric impulses can be sent through wires but to date our methods for transmitting messages have been very crude. One cumbersome device I examined recently used twenty-six wires, one wire for each letter of the alphabet, but my notion is to use only one wire and to indicate the letter by varying the length of the electric impulses and interpreting the results by means of a code."

Quentin tapped his forefinger on an open ledger, then sat at his desk. "This is my log book where I record my experiments."

Rodgers, who had remained standing, nodded. Glancing at the book and reading the listings upside down, one of his many useful skills, he noted that the last entry had been made more than three months before. It appeared that in the ten days since returning to town, Lord Devon had accomplished nothing.

Without preamble, Rodgers said, "Miss Riggs leaves town tomorrow for Gravesend. I believe she intends to reside there indefinitely, much to the distress of Mrs. Baldwin. And of myself."

Quentin sprang to his feet and paced back and forth in front of his desk. "Damnation," he muttered. "She intends to return to her star-gazing, I warrant. That young lady has a cursed stubborn streak. Will nothing bring her to her senses?" He paused. "How is she?" he asked, his voice suddenly tender.

"Unhappy with all of the gentlemen of the *ton,* or so she has declared." He had decided to say nothing about the unpleasantness involving Lord Alton.

Quentin sat down in his chair, raising both hands head-high in a gesture of hopelessness. Suddenly leaning toward Rodgers, he said, "I called on her shortly after she returned to London from the Manor, after I heard she had refused Gavin Spencer. She refused to see me. So I wrote to her only to have her return the letter unopened."

"I believe, my lord, that proud might be a more appropriate description of Miss Riggs than stubborn."

"Proud. Stubborn. The end result is exactly the same. Misery." He sighed. "When I thought she had accepted Spencer I spoke briefly with her at the masquerade ball and she may be under the impression I called her judgment into question. Perhaps she is still annoyed that I would ever think she would accept Spencer."

"Mr. Spencer," Rodgers said, "is reported to be readying another expedition."

"True enough. I was told at White's that at this moment he is gathering a crew of young gentlemen to sail to the eastern Mediterranean in a replica of an ancient Greek ship. When he arrives there he intends to recreate the heroic journey of Odysseus from Greece to Troy and home to Greece again."

"A journey which will certainly produce another exciting and informative book. I intend to reserve a copy at Mr. Cloverly's shop."

"Alicia Mallory." When Rodgers looked a question, Quentin shook his head, declining to explain his cryptic remark.

"Mrs. Baldwin and her friends," Rodgers said, "were exceedingly disappointed when Miss Riggs refused the overtures of Mr. Spencer, expecting her to give him a quite different answer. Now they seem to despair of ever finding a suitable gentleman for her."

Again Quentin stood, this time striding to one of his work tables. With a sweep of his hand he sent a jar of water hurtling to the floor where it smashed

241

into a hundred glittering pieces. Rodgers narrowed his eyes ever so slightly but made no comment.

Quentin came and put his hands palm down on the desk, leaning toward Rodgers. "Once," he said, "I truly believed that my work, this laboratory, my privacy and my freedom were the most important things in my life. Now I see this means nothing, nothing at all. Once I thought women were merely a distraction, a necessary evil. Now—" He shook his head, sighing. "It will not do, Rodgers, it will not do at all."

Rodgers suppressed a smile. "No, my lord," he said, "it will not do."

"She refuses to see me." Quentin scowled. "Perhaps not without reason from her perspective since I suppose I can be viewed as overbearing at times. There are even those, Alton for one, who have called me worse than that."

"He has indeed, my lord. Or so I have heard."

Quentin gave him a speaking look but plunged on. "As you must be aware," he said, "Miss Riggs has a habit of challenging me at every opportunity and in every conceivable way. This refusing to see me or read my letters is her latest challenge, I expect."

Rodgers nodded.

"Hers is a rather annoying habit," Quentin went on, "since she carries it to ludicrous extremes. She succeeds in becoming especially aggravating because she emerges victorious more often than not. I wish that once, only once, she would resist her urge to compete with me." Quentin sat once more in his chair. "Pray pardon my ranting, Rodgers. I mentioned her challenges because I was about to make a suggestion. I do believe I should turn the tables on her by issuing a challenge myself."

"Excellent. If I may be allowed to use a mixed metaphor, my lord, you will be throwing down the gauntlet and then waiting for her to rise to the bait."

"Exactly." Quentin leaned back in his chair, staring at the ceiling, deep in thought. "Now what shall my challenge be? You must help me decide."

"Allow me time to give the matter some thought," Rodgers said. "And also let me approach Miss Riggs and engage her in conversation so I may better judge the lay of the land."

"My fate, Rodgers, is in your hands. As soon as you ascertain the lay of the land I shall throw down the gauntlet and she, I sincerely hope, shall rise to the bait."

Justine gazed from the front parlor window of the Baldwin town house at the bustle on the street outside. A boy rolling a hoop by striking it with a stick ran along the walkway, a landau driven by a stout and pompous coachman rumbled past, a rabbit woman stood beside her cart crying her wares of fowl and small game.

Justine sighed. How she would miss London! The city pulsed with excitement, every new vista charmed her more than the one before, even the dirt and the dust and the smells, even the smoke and the fog failed to give pause to her enthusiasm. She had never felt more alive in her life.

Even more than the city, she would miss all those who had befriended her. That very afternoon they had gathered at the Baldwin house for tea to wish her farewell. Her eyes misted as she recalled each of them presenting her with a small gift of remembrance, a deck of tarot cards from Daphne, an assortment of fastening pins from Gerard (of his own unique design), a riding crop from Ogden, and an envelope from Prudence that she was cautioned not to open before she reached Gravesend.

She had been looking forward to returning to her small observatory at Gravesend but when, the night before, she had walked into the garden and looked up at the panoply of stars they seemed strangely cold and distant. Could it be that her enthusiasm for astronomy was waning?

Despite these nagging doubts, she was determined to leave on the morrow. She had made up her mind to go back to Gravesend and she would. She could not, however, suppress a sigh as her thoughts returned, as they did so often, to Quentin. Once more she pictured him riding out of the mist in Hyde Park, again she relived the moment he kissed her on Round Hill and recalled the magic of his embrace beneath the willow. With an angry shake of her head she tried to drive him from her mind.

"Miss Riggs."

Startled, she turned from the window to find Rodgers standing beside the marble-topped table, his hand resting lightly on the Bible.

Coming to her, he said, "I wanted to tell you how much all of the servants, but especially myself, will miss you."

Justine thanked him and, sitting, invited him to be seated but he demurred. When she insisted, he reluctantly perched on the edge of a chair near her, his hands folded in his lap, his kind hazel eyes watching her.

Suddenly she found herself telling him of her misgivings about returning to Gravesend, her frustrated hopes for a new life in London and her nagging fears that she might be making a mistake. When she finished he reached to her and pressed her hand between both of his.

"I bring you a message from Lord Devon," Rodgers said.

Her heart leapt.

"I went to him in his retreat on Whitechapel Road this morning," he told her, "which, by the by, is not what many suspect it to be. Lord Devon has built a laboratory there where he conducts experiments with something he terms a telegraph, a mechanical device for sending messages by means of electrical impulses carried on wires over considerable distances."

She gaped in surprise. A laboratory? Quentin had never hinted at such a thing. What else had he kept concealed from her? "His message?" she asked.

"He challenges you to a race on horseback over the distance of one mile," Rodgers went on, "a race to take place tomorrow morning in Hyde Park."

"He challenges me to a race?" Disappointed and confused, she shook her head. "No, I think not," she said.

Remembering how she had, from the first, constantly challenged Quentin, Justine felt a pang of guilt. Now, when she wanted something very different from him, he was offering *her* a challenge. Had he experienced a similar frustration when she was the challenger? Was this his revenge?

"Do you recall," Rodgers asked, "after we had that unpleasantness with Lord Alton you said you wanted to thank me in some way? You can—by agreeing to meet Lord Devon in the morning."

She frowned, puzzled. "My racing him would please you, Rodgers?"

"I believe in completing whatever one has left unfinished, in the tying off of loose ends. Have you noticed how much of life takes place in the form of circles, whether in the rotation of the Earth about its axis or the revolving of the planets around the sun or the arc of a man's life from the helplessness of infancy to the feebleness of old age? You came to us, to Mrs. Baldwin and myself, after you raced Lord Devon in the park, because you raced him, so it seems only right to me that you should leave us only after racing him again."

"You sound like a hopeless romantic, Rodgers. To me, most of life seems to consist of those dangling loose ends."

"It does, unfortunately. All the more reason to tie those that we can. So, yes, Miss Riggs, to answer your question, it would please me mightily if you accepted Lord Devon's challenge."

Justine placed her hand on his. "Then I shall," she promised. "For you, Rodgers."

The next day, as the first light of dawn shimmered on the rising wisps of the morning fog, she rode beside Rodgers to Hyde Park astride Fitzwilliam, a four-

246

year old chestnut, a gelding Rodgers swore was the equal of any horse in all of England. She wore the same jockey attire she had worn months before when she came to the park for her first fateful race against Quentin.

As they neared the agreed-upon meeting place, her heart pounded even though she had steeled herself against still another disappointment. She came here this morning, Justine told herself, only as a favor to Rodgers.

"This is where Lord Devon told me we would find him," Rodgers said as they reined in beneath a magnificent oak. He peered hopefully into the mist. "He planned to come with Mr. Willoughby, who may have delayed him," he added. "And we *are* somewhat early."

Time passed slowly for Justine. Rodgers made sporadic, halfhearted attempts at conversation but she said little in reply, telling herself that she should never have listened to Rodgers. No, be honest with yourself, Rodgers or no Rodgers, I would have come here this morning if only to see Quentin one last time.

Hearing hoofbeats, she glanced to her right and her breath caught as she saw him, saw Quentin, much as she had that first time, riding out of the mist. Rodgers said something; his words meant nothing to her. Another rider followed Quentin; she was only vaguely aware of his presence, she had eyes only for Quentin.

Justine rode toward him, saw him staring at her as though the sight of her had dazed him. She reined her horse to a halt; he stopped only a few feet away from her, his green eyes dark and intent. Suddenly he swung to the ground and reached up for her. Letting herself fall toward him, she felt his strong hands grip her about the waist and then he swung her to the ground. For a long moment they gazed into each other's eyes, neither of them speaking.

"I was lost without you, Justine," he said at last. "I could do nothing, I wanted to do nothing. I forgot to eat, I couldn't sleep without waking to thoughts of you, how terribly I missed you."

"Quentin," she murmured. Being with him was all she wanted. She would do anything for him, he had only to ask, if only she could be with him now and forever.

"Justine," he said. "Justine, Justine, Justine," he said, repeating her name over and over again. "I love you, Justine. Will you marry me?"

She gasped. For an instant speech failed her. "Oh, yes," she murmured, overcome with joy, "I think I loved you from the day we met."

She became aware of another voice, a man's voice, loud and insistent. Quentin, still holding her in his arms, turned his head.

"The race," John Willoughby said. "When shall we start the race?"

"The devil take the race," Quentin told him, obviously annoyed at the interruption. He looked at her. "Unless you—?" he began.

She shook her head. "From this day forward," she promised, "I intend to help you, not compete with you."

He drew her closer, his hand caressing her back as it slid up to the nape of her neck.

"For the most part," she added with a smile.

As he leaned to her, just before his lips found hers, Quentin said, "I wouldn't want it any other way."

Rodgers sat at a table in the Baldwin drawing room, his pen poised above the Society journal, as the four members of the Matrimonial Recruitment Society began their meeting.

Glancing from one Society member to another, Rodgers smiled to himself. As matchmakers, they had proven themselves to be complete and utter failures. Fate and love had brought Lord Devon and Justine together, not the misdirected efforts of the members of the Society. On the other hand, Rodgers was forced to admit, those efforts had produced a variety of unusual and rather wonderful side effects.

Although Prudence Baldwin still complained at times of alarming symptoms, she was quickly distracted by the ever-increasing attentions being paid her by Gerard Kinsdale. As for Gerard, he was now enjoying his first visit to London in many years. Rodgers had learned, from reliable sources on the Kinsdale staff, that Gerard had begun applying his undoubted talents to the refurbishing of both the grounds and house at Kinsdale Manor as well as directing his inventive genius into more practical channels.

Ogden Stewart still occasionally professed a disdain for women but the flirtatiousness of Daphne Gauthier had had a salutary effect in that Ogden spoke less and less of the glories of the past and more and more of the promise of the future, a future that Rodgers suspected might include a liaison with, if not marriage to, the vivacious astrologer.

Rodgers abandoned his musings and turned his attention to the meeting when he heard Daphne ask, "And when will Justine's marriage to Lord Devon take place?"

"On the week before Christmas," Prudence informed her. "After a short visit to Brighton, they plan a trip to Paris and the French Mediterranean coast."

"I do believe we can congratulate ourselves on the felicitous outcome," Gerard said. "Though for a time we considered Mr. Gavin Spencer to be the best prospect for Justine, we did set in motion the series of events, beginning with the eclipse party, leading to her betrothal and the happiness certain to follow her marriage to Devon."

Ogden cleared his throat. "Hear, hear," he cried, raising his glass. "I propose a toast to the Matrimonial Recruitment Society."

They touched glasses and sipped their wine.

"My only regret," Daphne said, "is that the engagement brings our work to an end."

"Must it be so?" Prudence glanced at the others. "Should we allow such a worthy activity to languish and die? There must be scores if not hundreds of other young ladies who could benefit from our assistance in finding the men of their dreams."

"How true." Gerard pursed his lips in thought. "Emeline Willoughby for one. And that other young lady who sang at our musical evening. What was her name?"

"Phillippa," Daphne told him. "And there are many, many more. We could ask Rodgers to make a list for us and then choose the one most in need of our assistance."

"God help us all," Rodgers murmured.

"What was that, Rodgers?" Ogden asked. "What did you say?"

Rodgers looked at him, an expression of pious earnestness on his face. "I was praying for the help of the Lord in your new endeavor," he said.

"Thank you, Rodgers," Ogden said, "we thank you, one and all."

A Memorable Collection of Regency Romances

BY ANTHEA MALCOLM AND VALERIE KING

THE COUNTERFEIT HEART   (3425, $3.95/$4.95)
by Anthea Malcolm
Nicola Crawford was hardly surprised when her cousin's betrothed disappeared on some mysterious quest. Anyone engaged to such an unromantic, but handsome man was bound to run off sooner or later. Nicola could never entrust her heart to such a conventional, but so deucedly handsome man. . . .

THE COURTING OF PHILIPPA   (2714, $3.95/$4.95)
by Anthea Malcolm
Miss Philippa was a very successful author of romantic novels. Thus she was chagrined to be snubbed by the handsome writer Henry Ashton whose own books she admired. And when she learned he considered love stories completely beneath his notice, she vowed to teach him a thing or two about the subject of love. . . .

THE WIDOW'S GAMBIT   (2357, $3.50/$4.50)
by Anthea Malcolm
The eldest of the orphaned Neville sisters needed a chaperone for a London season. So the ever-resourceful Livia added several years to her age, invented a deceased husband, and became the respectable Widow Royce. She was certain she'd never regret abandoning her girlhood until she met dashing Nicholas Warwick. . . .

A DARING WAGER   (2558, $3.95/$4.95)
by Valerie King
Ellie Dearborne's penchant for gaming had finally led her to ruin. It seemed like such a lark, wagering her devious cousin George that she would obtain the snuffboxes of three of society's most dashing peers in one month's time. She could easily succeed, too, were it not for that exasperating Lord Ravenworth. . . .

THE WILLFUL WIDOW   (3323, $3.95/$4.95)
by Valerie King
The lovely young widow, Mrs. Henrietta Harte, was not all inclined to pursue the sort of romantic folly the persistent King Brandish had in mind. She had to concentrate on marrying off her penniless sisters and managing her spendthrift mama. Surely Mr. Brandish could fit in with her plans somehow . . .

Available wherever paperbacks are sold, or order direct from the Publisher. Send cover price plus 50¢ per copy for mailing and handling to Zebra Books, Dept. 4441, 475 Park Avenue South, New York, N.Y. 10016. Residents of New York and Tennessee must include sales tax. DO NOT SEND CASH. For a free Zebra/Pinnacle catalog please write to the above address.